To Pola, my

The mindful adventures of
Master Owl ®

ROB HOLMES *B Holmes*

ILLUSTRATED BY BEIDI GUO

www.robholmes.org

The Mindful Adventures of Master Owl

Text copyright © 2021 by Rob Holmes

Illustration copyright © 2021 by Beidi Guo & Rob Holmes

ISBN 978-1-80068-004-3

First printed in Great Britain 2021.

The right of Rob Holmes and Beidi Guo to be identified as author and illustrator of this work has been asserted by them in accordance of the Copyright, Designs and Patents Act 1988.

All rights reserved. No part of this book may be used or reproduced by any means, graphic, electronic or mechanical, including photocopying, recording, typing or by any information storage retrieval system without the written permission of the author except in the case of brief quotations in bodied in critical articles and reviews.

This book and other titles by Rob Holmes can be ordered through book sellers or by contacting:

Remember Who We Are Publications

Two Barns, Idston, Kingsbridge, Devon TQ7 4EJ

www.robholmes.org

Dedicated to my children,
Sam, Lucy, William and Eddie
and to all the children on this beautiful planet
who deeply desire to live in peace with one another
and in harmony with all living things.

Wishing you many Magical Mindful Moments.

CONTENTS

1. IN THE BEGINNING

Deep in the forest live many different kinds of animals.

Badgers, mice, woodpeckers, squirrels, elephants, caterpillars, bears, butterflies, deer and foxes.

They are all working away, collecting food, making nests, building dams and being very, very busy.

But there is one animal who is different from the rest. He is a very wise and special owl. The other animals call him 'Master Owl'.

When he was growing up, he was just a normal owl, raised by his mum and dad and living with his sister and brother.

But he was different from the rest of his family. While they fluttered and squawked and jumped up and down, he liked to sit quietly on a branch, covered in comfy green moss. He didn't say much. There was something very peaceful about him.

He liked to watch all the other animals.

He liked the way the sunlight shone through the trees.

He enjoyed listening to the sound of the rain dripping off the leaves.

He loved the changing of the seasons.

The crunch of the snow in the winter under his feet.

The fresh lime green of new leaves in the spring.

The busy buzz of the bees in the summer.

The rustle of the autumn leaves in the wind.

He spent years enjoying the beauty of the forest, sitting peacefully on his branch. But one day, something amazing happened to him.

He felt like his whole body was being filled with golden sunlight. He was so happy and peaceful. His life was never the same again.

After this, the other animals began to notice there was something very different about this owl. He had a happy glow about him. When they moved close to him, they felt very peaceful.

Sometimes Master Owl was so relaxed sitting with his eyes closed, that he totally forgot where he was and fell off his favourite branch!

Down he fell . . . eyes still closed . . . until . . .

CLUNK!

He landed on the ground, making a big PUFF of leaves and feathers.

He never seemed to hurt himself. He was always OK.

He always laughed to himself when he fell off

his branch. He loved to chuckle. He didn't take himself at all seriously.

But he was very wise. If any of the animals had a problem and needed help, they always went to see him.

He always seemed to know how to help them.

He never knew what he was going to say.

The right words just came out.

2. MASTER OWL MEETS MISS BUNNY

Our story begins today as Master Owl is sitting quietly on his branch, as he loves to do. His eyes were closed. He found this helped him to hear better. He loved listening to the birds singing.

But today there was another sound, that was sitting behind the bird sounds. It was very quiet. He had to listen very carefully and tune into it. After a few moments, he knew what this sound was.

He could hear another animal gently sobbing.

He opened his eyes, spread his wings out wide and gracefully glided down through the trees. All the time he was listening to the crying sound, as it got louder and louder, until he reached the source of the sobs.

The noise was coming from an open window of small house, that was built into the side of a large bank.

He stuck his head through the window and said 'Hello ... hello... hello.' His words echoed down through the house.

'T-wit-ta-who's down there? I am Master Owl.'

'Come in Master Owl' came a sad voice from inside the little house.

Master Owl opened the small door and bent his head down, so that he didn't hit his head. Inside he saw Miss Bunny, sitting crying in her bed.

'Hello Master Owl. I am so sorry to disturb your peace' said Miss Bunny.

'You haven't at all Miss Bunny. How you are

feeling?' he said.

'I am feeling very sad today and I don't have any energy,' she replied.

The tears ran down her cheeks. She blew her nose into a tissue with a big PHARP!

'It's OK to feel sad sometimes and those tears must have needed to come out. Tears really don't like to be stored up.'

Miss Bunny kept crying. But after a few seconds she wiped her tears away.

'Thank you, it's really good to meet you,' she said, 'I do feel better after having a cry.' She even managed a little smile.

'It's good to meet you too Miss Bunny' the wise owl said. 'Come and sit next to me, we are going to take this mindfully.'

'What does 'mindfully' mean?' asked Miss Bunny, looking very confused.

'It means to pay attention to what is happening outside of you and what you are feeling inside right now. Come, I will show you' he said.

Master Owl ducked down again through Miss Bunny's front door and they both walked into the warm sunshine. He sat down, with his legs crossed and Miss Bunny did the same.

'So close your eyes and take a deep breath in,' he said. 'Hold it for a few moments and then let it all out slowly.

Then take another deep breath, hold it in and then let it out slowly. Feel your shoulders dropping down and relaxing.'

Miss Bunny felt herself sinking down into the soft leaves and started to relax.

'That's really good. Well done' he said. 'Our breathing happens naturally all day and all night, but we forget to notice it. So when we pay attention to our breathing, it is deeply relaxing.'

Miss Bunny kept her eyes closed and followed Master Owl's voice. He continued. 'Just notice the air moving in and out of your nose, with every breath.'

She breathed in ..... and..... out. She had never

ever noticed her breath moving in and out of her
nostrils before.

'Can you feel the earth under your feet?' asked
Master Owl.

Miss Bunny focused her attention on her feet.
She felt the leaves and the soil in contact with her
body. She had not noticed she was even sitting
down when she first came outside. Her mind was
too busy.

'The ground is wonderful at supporting you', he
said gently.

'Now' said Master Owl, 'can you hear the sounds
of the birds singing in the distance?'

Miss Bunny focused on her hearing. Sure
enough she heard the distant sound of birds
singing. She even heard the far off sound of a
woodpecker... TAP TAP TAP, tapping it's beak on
the trunk of a tree. She had not noticed any noises
before this magical moment.

They just sat and both listened for what seemed
like a long time. Hearing the sounds of the forest

all around them. So many different sounds. Some near and some far away.

Miss Bunny found this so relaxing, just listening to the sounds.

'Next' said Master Owl, 'can you smell the forest all around you?'

Rabbits have an amazing sense of smell, so Miss Bunny twitched her little nose. The first thing she noticed was the sweet smell of a pine tree. She had not noticed any smells when she first sat down with Master Owl.

She felt herself sink further down into the ground. Slowly a big, wide smile broke out across her face.

'How do you feel now?' asked Master Owl.

'Much better, thank you. My mind is less busy and I feel more peaceful' said a smiling Miss Bunny.

'That's wonderful' he said, 'I call this a Magical Mindful Moment or mmm for short!'

Master Owl picked up a stick and drew three

letter m's in the earth and made a mmmmmm sound.

'Mmmmmm!' laughed Miss Bunny, 'it really is very magical!'

'Miss Bunny' said Master Owl, 'close your eyes again. Can you understand why you feel sad at the moment?'

Miss Bunny was quiet for a short while. Then she suddenly opened her eyes, looking like she had made a big discovery.

'Yes, I know why I have been feeling so sad,' she said, 'I feel so lost and small in this huge wood. I feel like I am not important at all.'

'I see,' said Master Owl, 'so you feel sad when you believe you are separate and not connected to everything else in the wood? Is that right?'

'Yes' replied Miss Bunny.

'Well then, I am not surprised you feel sad!' said Master Owl, looking thoughtful. After a few moments he said.

'I have an idea that I think will help you.

Go out into the forest and dig little holes in the ground between the trees. I will come back in a week's time to see what you find.'

And with that, Master Owl patted Miss Bunny on her back and said,

'twit a see you soon!'

He flew off silently back into the woods towards his Home tree.

Miss Bunny sat there, looking confused, scratching her head.

'Digging holes between trees?' she thought to herself, 'what does he mean? How will that help me to feel part of the wood?'

Miss Bunny sat there for a few more minutes, enjoying the peace and then she went back into her house and came back out with a spade.

Even though Miss Bunny didn't understand why she should dig holes between the trees, she trusted Master Owl and started to dig.

Miss Bunny started digging one hole after another in the ground between the trees.

Everywhere you looked, there were piles of soil from all the digging. If you wanted to know where Miss Bunny was, then all you had to do was look for a hole with soil flying in the air. Miss Bunny worked her way down into the ground with her trusty spade, chucking the soil into big piles.

DIG. CHUCK. DIG. CHUCK. DIG. CHUCK.

Sometimes she covered up smaller insects, like beetles and snails, who were NOT happy to have soil piled on their heads. 'Bunny!', they shouted. 'Sorry' she replied.

And boy, did she dig a lot of holes! Hundreds of holes, everywhere!

One week later and true to his word Master Owl glided silently down off his favourite branch to go and see Miss Bunny.

She was waiting for him, with a big smile on her face. She was doing a dance!

'Hello you funny bunny' he said, smiling. 'You look much happier than when I last saw you. Did you find out anything in this last week?'

'Oh Master Owl, it's been an incredible week! I was so confused when you asked me to dig holes between the trees. I mean, what can I learn from digging holes? I am already the best animal in the wood at digging holes, better than badgers and moles! If there was a competition for digging holes, I would win!'

'So what happened Miss Bunny?' he asked.

She told her story.

'As I started digging, the first thing I hit with my spade was the root of a tree. So I kept digging and followed this root to see where it went. Then I discovered more tree roots and found that all the roots of the trees were touching each other. It's like the trees are holding hands under the ground! They give each other messages. It's amazing.

Trees look like they are standing alone in the wood, but from under the ground, they are connected together. If there is a big storm, then the trees help to support one another.

'That's amazing to find out. What else did you discover in the trees?' asked Master Owl.

Miss Bunny continued.

'I realised that the trees were homes to so many other animals. I met Mrs Woodpecker and she showed me her nest with baby birds.

I met Mr Squirrel and he showed me where he stored all his nuts. He explained how the acorns grow on the oak trees and how he collects them up, so he has enough food for the winter.

I met a huge family of buzzing bees and they showed me how they were all making honey.

Queen Bee explained that all the bees had different jobs. Some collected nectar. Some build the hives. Some look after the baby bees.

I met a family of deer, using the leaves of a tree to shelter out of the sun. Mrs Deer said that they would get too hot without the shade of the trees in the summer.

All the animals were really friendly to me, apart from Mr Squirrel, who was a bit grumpy.

Then I had another Magical Mindful Moment and realised that the trees help us to have lovely fresh air to breathe. Trees breathe in and out, in the same way we animals do.'

'Yes, this is very true' said Master Owl, 'the trees are very important for our world, but sometimes we are too busy to stop and notice how helpful and amazing trees really are. Did you notice anything else?'

'Yes' said Miss Bunny. 'After all that digging I was hungry, so I started to nibble a flower. I was really noticing how tasty this flower was, when I had a big 'ah ha' moment.'

'What did you realise?' asked Master Owl.

'I realised that this flower was only growing because of the bumble bees that visited the flower, helping a new flower to grow. The worms in the soil helped the little seed to grow in healthy earth. The rain and the sun made the flower grow big and strong.

Some kind of magic helps to make everything grow in the woods, including little old me!'

'That's right. How do you feel now?' asked Master Owl.

'Oh Master Owl' she said, 'I feel so happy now, because I feel connected to everything in this world. I have made new friends, like Mrs Woodpecker and Mrs Deer. And I have noticed how a magical energy runs through all living things. I don't feel alone anymore. In fact, I feel like everything in the forest is my family.'

'That's wonderful to hear Miss Bunny,' said Master Owl smiling.

'Thank you so much Master Owl,' she said, 'I

will take time every day to have more Magical Mindful Moments!'

'Mmmmmmm,' said the owl grinning, 'they're the best.'

'Can I please spend more time with you' she asked, 'there is so much to learn from you. Will you teach me?'

'Of course' he replied, 'I would be honoured. Come Miss Bunny, let's go and see who needs helping next.'

Master Owl flew through the trees and Miss Bunny hopped along on the ground, following him all the way back to his Home tree.

Miss Bunny knew she had come home. She started digging to make her new house in the roots of the tree where Master Owl lived.

This is how Miss Bunny met Master Owl. It's amazing how life can change in one magical moment, in the flap of a wing and the hop of a leg.

MASTER OWL'S WISE WORDS

Just like Miss Bunny, it's OK to feel sad sometimes. Crying can be very helpful. I think of tears as little drops of love. We cry because we care deeply.

Mindfulness gives us a chance to notice how we are feeling. Give your parents and other adults a chance to listen to how you are feeling. It's important they know how you are. A problem shared is a problem halved. Anything that we can talk about, we can manage to cope with.

When we are feeling stuck, doing some kind of physical exercise can really help. Miss Bunny felt much better for digging all those holes.

Have you noticed how everything in nature is linked? Next time you are out in nature, see if you can spot any connections between the flowers, trees, grass, plants and animals. It's good to take a 'Magical Mindful Moment' and notice nature.

Next time you are outside, just close your eyes and listen for the sounds all around you. It's a funny thing, but closing your eyes improves your hearing! If you don't believe me, try it for yourself!

3. THE GRUMPY CATERPILLAR

The time is half past five in the morning. It's dawn. The sun is rising slowly. Light returns to the wood once again.

The birds were up and singing their morning songs. No one really knew why they sang. Perhaps they were simply happy to be alive, so they sang.

Master Owl is also awake. He loves to sit quietly on his favourite branch and watch the sun coming up.

With his eyes closed, he loves hearing all the

birds starting to sing.

He notices it is always the robins who start singing first. Next it is the blackbirds, followed by a woodpecker. It is like an invisible conductor is guiding this wonderful choir every morning.

Master Owl feels a wonderful energy is guiding everything around him, including him. 'One magical movement of wonder,' he thinks to himself.

Meanwhile at the bottom of the tree, Miss Bunny is also awake. It has been a few weeks since she first met Master Owl. Since then, she had built herself a new house at the foot on his Home tree.

She is busy planning a little surprise for Master Owl. She worries about him falling off his favourite branch when he is being mindful. She does not want him to hurt himself. Therefore, she has a plan. She bought him a trampoline!

She places the trampoline on the ground, right below Master Owl's branch. Sure enough, a few minutes later, Master Owl is so relaxed, listening to all the birds sing, he falls off the branch!

Down he falls, with his eyes still closed shut.

Miss Bunny holds her breath. Her eyes are open wide. She is a little bit nervous to see what happens next.

Her teacher falls very quickly, down towards the ground, head first. He looks like a feather-covered coconut falling from a tree!

Master Owl lands in the middle of trampoline on his head and with a massive B - O - I - N - G, bounces all the way back up onto the branch. He lands back on his feet. He never even opens his eyes.

Miss Bunny could not believe her eyes!!

Master Owl opens his eyes and smiles. He was playing a game with his friend. He knew she had placed a trampoline under him. He thought he would fall off, to see what happened. That's the thing about being mindful. He was so aware of what was going on around him.

Master Owl trusted in life. He always landed on his feet (or his head), when he needed to.

'Thank you, Miss Bunny, for my bounce. It's a good reminder that life has it's little ups and downs' said Master Owl, 'can I join you for breakfast?'

'Yes of course you can', she replied. 'But how did you know about the trampoline?'

'I was listening carefully' he said 'so I heard you dragging it into position.'

Miss Bunny smiled and shook her head. He was a very special owl, with amazing ears!

Master Owl sometimes flew down to the base of the tree trunk to share breakfast with Miss Bunny. Rabbits are definitely happier being on the ground than up a tree.

Ever since the first day they met, Miss Bunny had decided to be his student.

She wanted to learn from him, because he was the wisest and kindest animal she had ever met. He was also funny. He didn't give a hoot what others thought of him. But he noticed everything, with those enormous eyes of his and big ears!

Master Owl noticed that Miss Bunny liked her breakfast to be exactly the same every morning. It wasn't just that she always had porridge with honey. The position of her fork, knife, bowl and cup were always the same.

Always in exactly the right place.

This morning, Master Owl moves around all her things before she arrived for breakfast, to see if she noticed. She did notice. She moves them all back into position!

'I like things staying the same' said Miss Bunny. 'It makes me feel safe and happy.'

Master Owl sits quietly eating his breakfast. He wonders how he might be able to teach Miss Bunny about change. About trying new things. About seeing what happens when we are brave.

Then, just as he is pondering this, a large and grumpy caterpillar crawls across the breakfast table.

They hear her saying, 'mess, mess, mess, always mess, blooming mess!'

'Good morning Mrs Caterpillar' said Master Owl kindly. 'Have you met Miss Bunny before?'

Miss Bunny said 'hello, lovely to meet you,' in a cheery voice.

'Hello you two' replied Mrs Caterpillar gruffly, 'sorry, but I haven't got time to stop and talk. Too much to do. Too much to sort out. Too much to tidy. Mess, mess, mess.'

She grumbles her way past them and heads off along the ground away from Master Owl's tree.

Master Owl looks at Miss Bunny.

Miss Bunny looks at Master Owl, with a knowing look in her eyes. They knew they could help.

They finish their breakfast and follow the grumpy caterpillar.

They don't have a problem keeping up with her, because she moves very slowly.

Miss Bunny watches her and counts her legs.

She has 16 legs.

Miss Bunny thinks it is funny how slowly she moves with 16 legs. If she had 16 legs, she would be the fastest animal in the wood!

And all the time, Mrs Caterpillar is muttering under her breath, 'mess, mess, mess, always in a mess.'

After what seems like a very long time, they arrive at Mrs Caterpillar's house, which is in a clump of dandelions.

She is so busy being grumpy, she doesn't noticed the owl and rabbit following her. She is too busy talking to herself to care.

'Mrs Caterpillar,' said Miss Bunny, 'can I ask why you are always saying 'mess, mess, mess.' What is in a mess?'

'My house' she replies, 'it's always a mess. The moment I tidy up, it gets messy again. Nothing stays the same. I just want it to stay the same.'

Master Owl gives Miss Bunny a knowing look and smiles.

'Yes, I am the same' says Miss Bunny. 'I like

things to be the same too. It's annoying when things get messy again.'

'It drives me CRAZY!' replies the caterpillar.

'Let me help you tidy,' said Miss Bunny helpfully.

Miss Bunny bends down and tries to help tidy Mrs Caterpillar's little house. This is not easy. As you might have realised, even small rabbits are a lot bigger than caterpillars!

Let's just say, it doesn't go well.

Miss Bunny breaks Mrs Caterpillar's little table. She knocks over her chairs. She pulls down her curtains. She make a big mess of the little house.

'Sorry' she said, 'I don't think I am helping very much.'

'Helping?!' replied a very cross looking caterpillar, 'now look at the mess! It's messier than ever. This will take me ages to tidy up.'

And with that, Mrs Caterpillar bursts into tears.

Master Owl always knew what to do next.

He puts his wing around Mrs Caterpillar and says 'we are here for you, so don't worry. Crying is good. Best to let those tears out. I guess you have been holding onto them for a long time.'

'Yes' said a very sorry looking Mrs Caterpillar, 'I think you are right Master Owl.' She blows her nose into a paper hanky and wipes her tears away.

'Can I make a suggestion' asks Master Owl, 'can the three of us all take a Magical Mindful Moment together?'

'A what?' said Mrs Caterpillar, looking confused.

'A Magical Mindful Moment', said Master Owl.

'I will explain.'

'We can get so busy sometimes, that we forget to notice this present moment, in the here and now. So, taking a mindful moment is magical, as you will see.

Let's all sit down together.'

Master Owl and Miss Bunny sit down with their legs crossed.

'I don't have to cross my legs, do I?' asks a

worried looking Mrs Caterpillar, 'it would take me a while, as I have 8 pairs of legs!'

Miss Bunny smiles and just about manages not to laugh out loud.

'No simply get comfortable,' said Master Owl. 'Let's close our eyes and start by taking three really good, long breaths in . . . and . . . out.'

All three animals breathe in . . . and . . . out and feel their shoulders relaxing and dropping.

'Notice the air moving in and out of your nose.

Notice how your tummy rises and falls.

Notice your body in contact with the ground.

Notice the sounds all around you,' said Master Owl.

Mrs Caterpillar already feels more relaxed.

She has never stopped and noticed her breathing before. She is normally too stressed and too busy trying to keep things just the same.

'Thank you, Master Owl,' she says, 'I am already starting to feel better. I have been so tired trying to keep everything tidy.'

'I understand that' said Master Owl, 'life is all about change. Let's look around us now at nature.

Do you see that really tall oak tree?'

Mrs Caterpillar nods.

'Do you think it was in a rush to grow that tall over the last hundred years?'

'No' said Mrs Caterpillar, 'it's growing little by little every year.'

'That's right' said Master Owl, 'and do you see the bud of that rose that is about to open?'

Mrs Caterpillar nods again.

'Is that flower in any hurry to open up?'

'No' says Mrs Caterpillar, 'it's opening when it's ready to.'

'Yes, in it's own sweet time' said the owl, 'do you like roses Mrs Caterpillar'

'Oh yes' she replies, 'I love the smell of roses and the colours of the petals.'

Master Owl continues. 'Imagine if I had a plastic

rose to give you. This fake rose never changed shape and didn't smell.

Then imagine I have a real rose with a beautiful smell, which blooms and then dies.

Which rose would you want to hold?'

'The real one' said Mrs Caterpillar with a smile.

In this Magical Mindful Moment, Mrs Caterpillar becomes calm and peaceful. She decides to stop trying to keep her life the same. She decides to let go and trust in change.

A few minutes pass.

Mrs Caterpillar gives the hugest yawn. She says she needs to go and have a really long sleep. She had never felt so tired in all her life.

'Rest well' said Master Owl, with a knowing look in his eye. 'Come on Miss Bunny, we will leave Mrs Caterpillar to have a long sleep.'

Master Owl and Miss Bunny return back to their Home tree.

For the first and only time in her life, Mrs Caterpillar starts to weave a cosy little sleeping bag. It is called a cocoon. When it is all finished, she settles down to sleep, with a happy smile on her face.

One week later, Master Owl said to Miss Bunny 'let's go and visit Mrs Caterpillar and see how she is doing.'

Miss Bunny has no idea what is going to happen next. Master Owl decides not to tell her. It will be a lovely surprise.

After arriving at Mrs Caterpillar's house, Miss Bunny is shocked to see this little cocoon jiggling and moving around.

'Master Owl, quick, let's help Mrs Caterpillar! She seems to be stuck in her little sleeping bag!' said a worried Miss Bunny.

'No Miss Bunny. Don't worry. We must leave her to get out on her own. It's really important that she struggles out on her own' said Master Owl.

Miss Bunny looks very confused. She has no

idea what is going on, but as always, she trusts her teacher.

They both keep their eyes fixed on the cocoon.

After much wriggling, there was a magical moment that Miss Bunny would never forget for the rest of her life.

Out of a small hole in the cocoon appears a flash of beautiful colours. First one wing appears. Deep reds, bright blues and a splash of yellow. Then a second wing and out comes Mrs Butterfly!

Miss Bunny is so surprised!!

'What's happened to Mrs Caterpillar?' says Miss Bunny, 'she's changed into a beautiful butterfly! How on earth did that happen?'

Master Owl smiles and says, 'she simply let go of thinking she was a caterpillar. She trusted in change.'

Miss Bunny stares at Mrs Butterfly, with her mouth wide open in wonder.

'Sometimes,' said Master Owl, 'we must be willing to let go of the life we planned, so that we can have the life that is waiting for us.'

After a few moments of drying her new wings in the sunshine, Mrs Butterfly looks at the owl and rabbit.

'Hello' she said, 'have we have met before? You look familiar.'

'Hello Mrs Butterfly' said Master Owl, 'it's lovely to meet you. I am Master Owl and this is Miss Bunny.'

The Butterfly just stares at them for a few moments.

'Oh yes, I do remember you!' said Mrs Butterfly, with a big smile on her face.

'I had the strangest of dreams. I dreamt I was a BIG green caterpillar! How funny. Dreams can seem so real. Then you wake up and realise it was only a dream!'

Master Owl and Miss Bunny look at each other and Miss Bunny winks at her teacher!

'Thank you so much for being here at this magical moment,' says Mrs Butterfly.

She flaps her new wings with such excitement. The warmth of the sun dries them out. She is ready to fly.

'Goodbye you two' she says, 'hope to see you again soon.'

And with that, Mrs Butterfly flies off into the sunshine to find some flowers. She is really hungry. It is time for her first breakfast.

Master Owl and Miss Bunny head back to their Home tree for breakfast.

Miss Bunny moves all her plates and cutlery around and laughs about it! She says she likes change and wants new adventures to unfold, just like they did for Mrs Butterfly.

Master Owl smiles and nods his wise head.

MASTER OWL'S WISE WORDS

It's natural to want life to stay the same, especially when we are happy. But the people in our lives are changing all the time. We are changing all the time. New things happen that we did not expect. Life is always changing around us.

But some things don't change. We are always aware of our experience. We always notice things and this never changes.

When we take a magical moment to breathe in this Now moment, we can connect with that part of us that is always calm and peaceful.

Sometimes there are big waves on the ocean when a storm rages, but deep down in the depths of the ocean, it's always still and calm.

Just close your eyes and take three slow, deep breaths in and out through your nose.

You will discover this inner calm. It's always waiting for you. Whatever age you are, it's always there. Like a silent friend, waiting to give you a hug.

4. THE CLUMSY BEAR

Some animals in the forest are stressed and very busy. Like Mrs Caterpillar, who rushed around all day trying to keep her little house tidy.

Some animals are lazy and don't do anything at all. They sit around waiting for something to happen.

And some animals are right in the middle of being busy and lazy.

Mr Bear is busy and lazy, which makes him extremely clumsy.

Today he is attempting to collect some honey from a bee's nest, high up in a tree. It is well known that bears love honey, but Mr Bear is always in such a rush. As a result, he is not very successful at collecting the golden nectar. Totally rubbish, in fact!

Mr Bear sees the bee's nest. He hears the buzzing of the bees. And he smells the sweetness of the honey with his big twitching nose. However, he is down on the ground and the nest is fifty feet up a tall tree. He wonders what to do.

Other animals might stop and think carefully about how to climb the tree.

Mr Bear is not one of those animals!

First he starts to climb up the tree trunk, hugging it, trying to find enough branches to stand on. But like most tree trunks, there are not enough branches on the lower part of the trunk, so Mr Bear got about a metre off the ground and slid back down onto his big furry bottom. He left 20 long scratch marks in the bark, as his finger and toe nails dragged down the tree trunk.

Next he fetches a ladder. He is sure this is going to work. But because he is what his mother calls 'slap-dash', he gets half way up the ladder when it slides off the side of the tree trunk. The ladder and Mr Bear collapse to the ground in a puff of leaves.

Next he fetches a rope, throws it over a branch and starts to pull himself up. However, there are two problems. Firstly, Mr Bear is really heavy. Secondly, the branch he is using for the rope is not strong enough. It breaks off, sending Mr Bear and the rope back to the forest floor. BOOF!

Then he has a brainwave and fetches a small trampoline. He feels sure this will work. He positions the trampoline under the honey tree and then takes a long run up. He runs as fast as he can, which to be honest is not very fast. He could have been overtaken by a caterpillar!

With all his might he jumps onto the trampoline. But the canvas is not strong enough to hold his weight! He rips a huge hole in the trampoline and once more, finds himself on the floor.

He is no closer to the honey.

Finally, he went out and bought himself a pair of special tree climbing boots. They have spikes in them, which stick into the bark. This had to work, he thought to himself.

He starts well, managing to get some distance off the ground. But his hands slip off the tree trunk. His boots stick in the bark. He ends up hanging upside down, looking like an enormous hairy fat bat!

At this point, he gives up and decides to look for another tree with a bee's nest, that is much easier to climb.

Talking of trees, back at Master Owl's Home tree, the wise owl and his apprentice, Miss Bunny have just sat down to have breakfast together.

'Can you please pass the honey?' asks Miss

Bunny.

Master Owl passes the honey pot, but sadly it is empty.

'That's a shame' said Miss Bunny, 'I wish there was more honey.'

Suddenly, there is a huge crashing sound coming from above and down falls a bee's nest onto the breakfast table. It covers everything in sweet sticky honey.

'Be careful what you wish for Miss Bunny! The Universe is always listening!' says Master Owl laughing.

As they are wondering why a bee's nest has fallen onto them, they look up and see a large bear. He is sliding down the tree trunk, looking a little embarrassed.

'Morning Mr Bear,' says Master Owl, 'nice of you to drop in!'

Miss Bunny laughs. She loves Master Owl's sense of humour.

'I am so sorry about the bee's nest ruining your

breakfast' said a very sorry looking bear.

'It's OK' said Miss Bunny, 'I was out of honey, but now there is lots to eat, so thank you.'

'Come and join us Mr Bear, for a spot of breakfast,' said the owl, 'it looks like you could do with a rest.'

Mr Bear slides down the rest of the tree and joins Master Owl and Miss Bunny for some bread and plenty of honey. Thankfully the bees have already left to start making a new nest.

As they sit there eating, Master Owl asks Mr Bear if he was happy.

'Happy? Not sure really' he replies, 'I am too busy to think about whether I am happy. I just rush around trying to collect honey and I never have time to stop and think. Rush, rush, rush.'

This reminds Miss Bunny of their old friend Mrs Caterpillar who was always so busy. She asks 'does it work for you, rushing around all the time?'

Mr Bear thinks carefully and then replies, 'not really, no. I am so clumsy and keep hurting myself.

I don't even rest in the winter, like most of my bear friends do.'

'Perhaps after breakfast, you would like to join me and Miss Bunny for a Magical Mindful Moment?' said Master Owl.

Mr Bear looks confused. 'I have no idea what you are talking about' he said.

'You'll see' says Miss Bunny 'most animals have never heard of Magical Mindful Moments. I hadn't until I met Master Owl.'

'Let's all sit together quietly' said Master Owl, as he flies down to the ground.

Miss Bunny and Mr Bear climb down the tree and sit down on the ground. They all cross their legs and get comfortable.

'Let's start with taking some deep breaths. Slowly breathing in through your nose and then letting the breath out through your nose,' said Master Owl.

'As you breathe in, think to yourself 'I know I am breathing in,' as you take in a breath and 'I know I am breathing out' as you let the breath out.'

They all took some slow, deep breaths together.

'Now let's take a moment to listen to the sounds around us' said Master Owl.

Mr Bear hears some distant bee's buzzing. He hopes it wasn't the bees he met this morning. They might be in a bad mood. Nope, the buzzing is getting more and more distant. Next he hears the sounds of a small stream trickling water over some rocks.

He feels himself settle down into his body. Normally his mind is so busy, he totally forgets about his body. This explains why he is always falling off ladders, crashing through trampolines and falling out of trees!

Mr Bear has never noticed the sounds around him before. He has never noticed the feeling of his legs in contact with the soft leaves under him.

He felt himself melting into the sounds and smells of the forest.

This certainly is a Magical Mindful Moment for

Mr Bear.

After what seems like hours of sitting quietly together, Mr Bear opens his eyes and looks around. Everything looks different to him. Then he realises the reason the wood looks different is because he feels differently inside. His mind is much less busy. In fact, he wasn't really thinking at all. There was now a quiet kind of peace.

He silently gazes around the wood. He sees the first snow flakes, drifting gently to the ground. One melts on his nose. Winter is coming.

'Thank you Master Owl and Miss Bunny, for bringing me home to myself' said a much calmer Mr Bear.

'You are very welcome' said Master Owl, 'all I did was to guide you back to the still, peaceful place that is always there inside you.'

Miss Bunny said 'I see our thoughts now, like waves on the ocean, rising and falling. But deep down in the depths of the ocean and inside us, there is a peace that is always there. Unchanging.'

Master Owl smiles when he hears Miss Bunny say this. She is an excellent student and is learning so much from him. Although he didn't think he was really teaching her anything new. More a case of reminding her to notice the peace and silence that moves through all things.

'My friends' said Mr Bear, 'I am not sure what has happened to me, but for the first time in my life I feel this strange urge to go and rest for the winter in a cave.'

Mr Bear says his good-byes and hugs his new friends. He heads off to find a cave to hibernate in for the winter.

Miss Bunny watches him leave. She notices that rather than rushing, he is walking slowly. He is taking in all the sounds and sights around him.

Watching the snow flakes fall is very relaxing. Miss Bunny thought snow flakes were always having a Magical Mindful Moment.

'Come Miss Bunny' said Master Owl, 'let's head back to our tree and leave Mr Bear to find his Dream Cave.'

'Dream Cave?' said Miss Bunny, 'I have never heard of a Dream Cave before.'

'Yes, it's very helpful to day-dream sometimes' said Master Owl.

'Why?' said Miss Bunny.

'Because when we take time to day dream and be quiet, it's much easier for new ideas to reach us' he replied.

He continues, 'if our minds are busy all the time thinking, then we can't hear the words of wisdom that the Universe is whispering to us.'

Miss Bunny takes a quiet moment, but all she hears is her tummy gurgling because she is hungry.

'I listened' she said 'and all I imagined was eating more honey!'

Master Owl laughs and they continue their journey home to their tree.

The snow continues to fall and the winter sets in. The streams freeze over and the forest is covered in a peaceful blanket of soft snow.

Meanwhile, tucked up warm and snug in his

cave is Mr Bear. For the first time in his life, he sleeps and dreams all winter long.

There is one dream that he keeps having. He dreams of building his own house, full of honey all stored in little pots.

This wonderful dream keeps him happily asleep for the rest of the winter.

Then one spring morning, as the snow melts, Mr Bear wakes up.

He emerges from his Dream Cave into the warm spring sunlight. He gives a huge yawn and stretches out his arms. He has been asleep for months, so he is very stiff and very hungry!

The news soon reaches Master Owl and Miss Bunny, that Mr Bear is awake. They hear he is much calmer now, less clumsy and feeling very happy with life.

The word in the woods is that Mr Bear had a dream about building a very special house.

Many of the other animals didn't believe the story about Mr Bear, because they knew him as the clumsy, busy bear. But Master Owl and Miss Bunny had seen the change come over him back in the autumn.

When Mr Bear's house is finished, he sets off to find his mindful friends. He wants to invite them over for tea.

Master Owl and Miss Bunny are excited to see their new friend. Miss Bunny secretly hopes there will be honey involved! She does have a very sweet tooth. Her mother was always giving her sweet foods when she was growing up!

Miss Bunny is not disappointed when she sees Mr Bear's house.

In fact, she is so surprised by what she sees that she can hardly speak!

It is a beautiful looking round house, with a little roof and chimney. But it was not the shape of the house that caught her eye. It was the six tiny little square boxes that were attached to the outside of the house.

'Hello Mr Bear' said Miss Bunny, 'what a fantastic new home, but what on earth are those little boxes on the outside of your house?'

'They are little houses for the bees, called bee hives' said Mr Bear with a smile.

Miss Bunny is amazed. She had never seen bee hives before, only bee nests high up in trees.

'You built a big house for you and six little houses for the bees' she said, 'but how did you dream up the idea to do this?'

'Well' said Mr Bear, 'as I was hibernating over the winter in my Dream Cave, I kept having the same dream about building my own house with these bee hives attached to the outside.

In my imagination I could see the whole design. Before this winter, my mind was always so busy I didn't make any time for new ideas to reach my mind. Now I daydream for a short while every day.

It's my own little Magical Mindful Moment.'

'Can we see inside please?' said Master Owl.

The three animals walk into Mr Bear's new house. Inside there are pots of honey sitting under 6 little taps, coming out of the wall.

'In my dream' said Mr Bear, 'I had this vision of building my house with bee hives attached to the outside wall. There is a little pipe coming through the wall and a tap. Now I can take some of the honey without disturbing the bees.'

Miss Bunny remembered the whole bee's nest falling down on their breakfast table the year before.

Mr Bear continues, 'so now I can take as much honey as I like and the bees are much happier too. We are a team now.'

'The bears and the bees' said Miss Bunny in wonder, 'working together in harmony – that's amazing.'

Mr Bear says, 'yes and that's all because of Master Owl's help in reminding me to take a moment to stop and breathe. I have realised the Universe is always whispering to us. All we have to do is stop and listen.'

'Would you like a pint of honey to take away for your breakfast?' asks Mr Bear.

'Thank you very much, but only a half pint for me please! I couldn't carry any more than that' replies a very grateful Miss Bunny.

Mr Bear took a little glass pot, went up to one of the honey taps and pours out half a pint of delicious golden honey. He gives it to Miss Bunny.

They say their goodbyes to Mr Bear.

Master Owl flies back home. Miss Bunny hops along, making sure she doesn't spill any of the honey.

When no-one is looking, she puts her paw in the top of the jar and has a little honey.

Back at Master Owl's Home tree, Miss Bunny is enjoying a honey sandwich. Master Owl wonders if some of the honey has been spilt on the way back from Mr Bear's house, as there is already quite a bit missing! He knew where the honey had gone. Miss Bunny's tummy!

'I am going to sleep now and I hope I have some amazing dreams' said Miss Bunny with a large yawn.

'Good night my friend. Dream well,' said Master Owl.

He goes out onto his favourite branch to sit peacefully. To him, this experience of being an owl living in a wood was all part of some fantastic dream.

He smiles as he sits silently and enjoys the silence and peace of the night.

The moonlight shines through the trees and up in the night sky, shooting stars whizz by.

It was magical.

MASTER OWL'S WISE WORDS

The Universe is always whispering ideas to us. We just need to take a moment to stop and listen.

Daydreaming can be very productive. In fact doing nothing can be one of the most productive things we do, because we are resting and enjoying the present moment. New ideas and insights are more likely to be noticed when we daydream.

Imagine trying to push a stick through a spinning fan. It would get chopped up. But when the fan is switched off, the stick passes through the still fan blades with ease. Our busy thinking minds are like a fast spinning fan. New ideas are like the stick, trying to reach us. So a Magical Mindful Moment allows us to receive new ideas and inspiration.

Animal Hospital

5. THE KiND DEER

It is a beautiful sunrise in the wood. Soft orange light filters through the leaves on the trees. A low mist hangs about on the forest floor. The birds are starting to wake up and sing their morning chorus.

In a clearing of trees stands a very nervous looking deer. She is standing very still, her ears alert, listening for the sounds of any danger.

Miss Deer is scared of pretty much everything. If she treads on a branch and it snaps, she runs away and hides.

If a pine comb falls from a tree, she jumps up in the air, terrified.

Once she was even scared by a loud rumbling sound, until she realised it was her own hungry tummy!

Poor Miss Deer.

Always alert.

Always worried.

But today, her life is about to change in a way she could never have imagined.

Miss Deer is nibbling on some grass in the clearing of trees when she hears a strange sound. It is an animal whimpering in pain. She looks in the direction of where the sounds are coming from. She is surprised to see a large grey wolf, lying on the ground, obviously upset and injured.

Her first reaction is to run away as fast as possible, because wolves kill deer, but she remembers what her friend Master Owl had once taught her about stopping and breathing.

He called it a Magical Mindful Moment.

They had met a few months before when Master Owl was out exploring the forest with Miss Bunny.

Like all the animals Master Owl and Miss Bunny met, Miss Deer had never heard of Magical Mindful Moments before.

She is very grateful to remember in that moment what Master Owl had taught her. She stops and takes three deep breaths in and out. This calms her down a lot. It really was a magical moment, because instead of feeling fear, she felt a wave of kindness come over her, seeing this poor animal in pain.

She slowly goes up to the wolf and sees that its leg is bleeding from an injury. Without thinking, she finds some soft leaves and stringy ivy and bandages up the wolf's leg.

Not only was this a life changing moment for Miss Deer but also for this wolf.

Mr Wolf had been taught by his mum and dad that deer was a source of food. But he had never seen this amount of kindness from another animal. Especially from an animal he would normally have chased and killed.

'Thank you so much for helping me' said Mr

Wolf, 'but why are you helping me?' he asked, looking very confused.

Miss Deer thought for a moment and then said 'I am as surprised as you are. All my life I have been taught to run away from wolves.'

'So what happened today?' asked Mr Wolf.

'My first thought was to run away,' she replied, 'but then I took a few deep breaths and thought about how much pain you were in. I couldn't leave you in this state. I wanted to help you.'

'I do really appreciate your help. Thank you,' said Mr Wolf.

'You are very welcome,' she said, 'I am happy to be able to help you.'

Miss Deer spent the next few days checking on Mr Wolf, changing his bandages, until he felt strong enough to return to his pack.

'Thank you, Miss Deer,' he said, as he walked home to find his family, 'I will never forget your kindness.'

Miss Deer went back to grazing on the grass that

only grew in the clearing between the trees. She is still on high alert for danger, but something has changed in her. She didn't know what happened to her when she first saw Mr Wolf, but something wonderful had happened.

One week later, Miss Deer is busy munching grass, while her ears keep a listen out for any sounds of danger. Suddenly she hears the snap of a twig on the ground near her. She looks up and is shocked to see another wolf walking slowly towards her. It wasn't Mr Wolf.

She thought about running away, when she hears the wolf say, 'Miss Deer, please help me. I am Mr Wolf's brother. He said you could help me.'

Miss Deer walks slowly and carefully towards the wolf. As she gets closer to him, she can see his ear is bleeding. It looks very painful.

'You have hurt your ear,' she said.

'Yes, I caught it on the sharp end of a broken

branch' he replied. 'My brother told all the wolf pack about how you had bandaged up his leg. He said you were the kindest animal he had ever met.'

She looks at the blood dripping slowly from the wolf's ear.

'Come over here' she said to the wolf, 'that ear of yours needs urgent help to stop it from bleeding.'

She fetches some special leaves called Aloe Vera and straps them to the wolf's injured ear. Miss Deer knew that different plants in the wood helped to heal wounds or illness.

After a few hours, the wolf is ready to leave.

'Thank you, Miss Deer' said the wolf, 'you really are amazing.' Miss Deer smiles and waves as he trots back to his pack.

The weeks and months go by.

The news about the kind deer spreads around the whole woodland community. More and more animals come to her with injuries and issues. Miss Deer is not scared anymore. So many animals ask for help. Many of these animals are ones that she would have run away from in the past.

Miss Deer makes a decision.

She starts up a hospital for sick animals.

There were too many animals coming to her for help and she needed support. Now the animals had a place they come to and receive help from Miss Deer and other nurses.

Meanwhile, in another part of the forest, another animal is trying to be kind. It is Miss Bunny.

Every morning, at dawn, Master Owl loves coming out onto his favourite branch. He found himself experiencing peace all the time, but he particularly loved the quietness of the dawn and dusk.

He closes his eyes and takes some long, deep breaths in. He becomes aware of all the sounds around him. He feels the bark under his feet. He smells the sweetness of a nearby pine tree. He notices his breath moving in and out of his nose.

Quite often, Master Owl is so peaceful that he falls backwards off his branch and lands in a clump of leaves on the ground. Miss Bunny didn't like it when this happened, so this morning she decided to take matters into her own paws.

She creeps silently onto Master Owl's meditation branch and attaches strong elastic to both his legs!

Having attached the elastic cords to Master Owl's legs, she goes back down the tree. She waits on the ground to see what will happen. A little cheeky smile creeps across her face!

But Master Owl knows exactly what was happening because he has heard Miss Bunny moving along his branch. He keeps his eyes closed and plays along with the game.

After a short while, Master Owl decides it is time to entertain Miss Bunny. Eyes still closed, he falls backwards off the branch. He falls down almost as far as the ground. Then with one enormous

S P R I N G of the elastic, he bounces back all the way up onto his branch. He never even opened his eyes.

Miss Bunny couldn't believe her eyes. Master Owl was back exactly where he started!

Master Owl slowly opens one eye and starts laughing. Miss Bunny realises she had been fooled by the wise, all knowing owl. She runs back inside and up the tree and appears next to Master Owl.

'How did you know I had attached the elastic cords?' asks Miss Bunny.

'Because' he replies, 'I can hear you. I can smell you. I can feel you on the branch and because I simply knew. This is what a Magical Mindful Moment feels like. It makes us feel very alive.'

'Sorry' said Miss Bunny, 'I hope you are not cross with me?'

'Cross? Of course not Miss Bunny, I think it's funny and very kind of you to think of me' says the owl smiling. He continues, 'but there is no need to worry about me. If I fall off, I am always OK and don't forget, I can fly if I need to!'

'Oh yes, I keep forgetting you are a bird!' says a relieved Miss Bunny, 'thank you Master Owl, you have taught me to always be kind to the other animals. I was practicing your teachings on you.'

'That's good, keep practicing kindness' he says. 'I have learned a lot about the importance of kindness from many animals in the wood. But the most amazing example is the kindness I saw practiced by that very gentle deer we met last year.'

'Do you mean Miss Deer?' asks Miss Bunny.

'Yes' said Master Owl.

'I remember you taught her about the wonders of Magical Mindful Moments. But in what way is she so kind?' enquires Miss Bunny, quite confused.

Master Owl starts telling the story of what happened when Miss Deer met the wolves.

Miss Bunny listens to every word from Master Owl's beak. He is an excellent story-teller.

'Wow' said Miss Bunny, with her mouth wide open in surprise, 'that's an amazing story. Miss

Deer overcame her fears and discovered such kindness for others, especially to her enemies, the wolves.'

'Yes and this was the start of something very beautiful. Come Miss Bunny, let's go and meet Miss Deer again. It's been too long since we last saw her.'

Miss Bunny unties the elastic from Master Owl's legs. They would not have got very far away with the elastic still tied on! She climbs onto Master's Owl back and off they fly through the woods.

It is quite a long journey.

When they arrive, Miss Bunny jumps off the owl's back. She looks at a gate with a modest sign above that reads 'Animal Hospital'.

There is a little bell by the sign. Master Owl rings the bell. To his delight, Miss Deer comes out of the hospital front door.

'Hello Master Owl and Miss Bunny' said Miss Deer, 'how wonderful it is to see you both again.'

'Thank you, Miss Deer,' replied Master Owl, 'it

was time I came to see you and visit your wonderful hospital. Miss Bunny has never visited before.'

'Hello again Miss Deer' said Miss Bunny, 'Master Owl has told me how this all started when you helped a wolf who was injured.'

'Yes' she smiled, 'that was a long time ago, but I can still remember it so clearly. One moment I was so frightened to see this scary animal. Then I remembered to breathe and have a mindful moment. Suddenly I found myself walking over to the wolf and realising he was hurt. Something happened in that moment. I felt such love for him.'

'Wow' said Miss Bunny, 'that's amazing and now you run a hospital for sick animals?'

'Yes, I seem to be' said Miss Deer smiling, 'and I am very grateful to Master Owl for his support in my work.'

Miss Bunny looked at her teacher, with an inquisitive look. She wondered how else Master Owl had helped Miss Deer.

Master Owl picked up on that and said, 'yes that's right. Do you remember when you first opened your hospital, the injured and sick animals would arrive so anxious and worried?'

'Yes' said Miss Deer, 'and that's when Magical Mindful Moments saved the day.'

Miss Bunny asks, 'how did Magical Mindful Moments help the sick animals?'

Miss Deer explains what happens at the hospital.

'The first thing we do is to bandage up any wound or injury. Then I sit with the animal. We close our eyes together and take some slow deep breaths.

Sometimes the animals start to shake, but this is simply the fear they felt at the time of the accident, starting to leave their bodies. It's actually a really healthy sign that healing has begun. It does not do us any good at all to hold on to that shaky energy. Better to let it out as soon as possible.'

Miss Bunny is all ears with her eyes wide open. She is learning so much from this beautiful deer.

Miss Deer continues, 'once the injured animals have relaxed a little, I ask them to keep focusing on their breath moving in and out of their bodies. I remind them that there is a difference between feeling pain and suffering from the pain.'

'I didn't know there was a difference' said Miss Bunny, curiously.

'Yes, there is quite a big difference' Miss Deer explains, 'when our bodies are injured in any way, they let us know by sending a pain message to our brains. You could think of it this way – it's our body's way of talking to us, so that we get the message to look after our bodies better!

The pain message is a natural and very helpful response. But then we have a choice on whether we suffer with this pain. Suffering is another layer that we apply to our lives. It all depends on how we judge the things that happen to us.'

'Oh I see' said Miss Bunny, 'that makes sense. Last time I hurt myself, I ran into a tree and hurt my head. I was really cross at myself for not seeing the tree in time and being in a hurry. I felt bad for days afterwards.'

'And there is another way of looking at this event,' said the wise deer. 'You had an accident and life gave you an opportunity to learn from it. Like taking things a bit more slowly. Every so called 'accident' is actually giving you a gift of learning.'

Master Owl comments too, 'so Miss Deer, what happens to your patients, once you have these Magical Mindful Moments with them and help them to see the gift?'

'Well, that's the wonderful thing' said Miss Deer smiling, 'the animals get better much more quickly when they rest, relax and forgive themselves. So much better than making a complete drama out of it!'

Master Owl then asks Miss Deer to tell Miss Bunny about what she has learned most from running her Animal Hospital.

'When I first told my family I was going to help look after sick and injured animals, including big scary ones like the wolves, they told me I was crazy. But I did it anyway.

I learned not to judge the other animals because of the way they looked. We never know what that animal has gone through. Often the animals that come to my hospital have been through really difficult times. My job is simple – love them anyway.'

Miss Bunny smiles and thanks Miss Deer for showing them around her hospital. They all give each other a big hug. Master Owl and Miss Bunny head back to their Home tree.

Miss Bunny was thinking about meeting this wonderful deer.

She said to Master Owl, 'thank you so much for taking me to meet Miss Deer again and see her amazing hospital. Her kindness has really inspired me.'

'Love them anyway,' she said, 'I love that!'

'Yes,' smiled Master Owl, 'that my rabbit friend, is perhaps the greatest lesson to learn in your life.

It's not always easy to love others, especially if they are nasty and unkind to you, but remember, all that means is that they have had a difficult life. They are probably hurting inside, so help them anyway.

At the end of the day, they are still part of your wider family, so love them anyway. Love has a magical way of bringing us all together.'

Master Owl and Miss Bunny sat together on the branch in the gentle dusk light and listened to the sounds of the forest animals settling down to sleep.

It had been another amazing day in the forest.

MASTER OWL'S WISE WORDS

  It's natural to feel fear sometimes, especially when we do something for the first time. At times the fear is there to remind us to look after our bodies. This is all fine. But amazing things can happen when we push outside of our safe comfort zone.

FEAR could stand for: Feeling Excited And Ready!

We can always choose to be kind to people. If people are not kind to us, then just show them how to be kind. Maybe no-one has ever shown them kindness before and all they needed was YOU to show them.

If someone upsets you and you can't think of anything kind to say to someone, then don't say anything. Words can stick with people, like an arrow sitting on a target, so best to keep unkind words inside you.

If you are feeling upset with someone, then take 5 minutes to have a Magical Mindful Moment. It will help you to feel calmer again.

Kindness is a super power!

6. THE FIBBING FOX

Miss Bunny is standing outside the front of her little house, which is set in the roots of Master Owl's Home tree.

It is a cute little house.

A large tree root curls up like a wooden arch and in the space below is Miss Bunny's front door, a perfectly round little door. Either side of the door are two little windows and a small chimney coming out of the roof.

Miss Bunny loves her new house, but most of all she loves learning from Master Owl. Every time they meet another animal, he shares his wisdom with them and changes their lives.

He reminds his fellow animals that there is a way to move out of their very busy thinking minds and have Magical Mindful Moments.

But this morning, Miss Bunny is not having a mindful moment at all.

She is very distracted and annoyed.

'Maybe Master Owl can be peaceful all the time,' she thinks to herself, 'but I am not feeling peaceful right now!'

She looks at her watch, again, for the ninth time in about three minutes and says under her breath, 'he's late - AGAIN!'

Master Owl is out on his favourite branch, as usual, being at peace with the world. But when he hears Miss Bunny's frustration, he opens his eyes and flies down to the ground to see her.

'Good Morning Miss Bunny' he said, 'you seem

a little agitated today – who's late again?'

Miss Bunny let out a big sigh. 'Sorry to disturb you Master Owl. Mr Fox is late, again. He is meant to be coming to mend my front door, but he is so unreliable.'

'Would you like to take a few mindful breaths with me?' said the always calm owl.

'Yes please' replied Miss Bunny, 'my mind is spinning like crazy.'

Master Owl guides his apprentice to sit down, close her eyes, take three really deep breaths and feel her shoulders sinking down with each breath.

It didn't take long before Miss Bunny felt herself relax back into her body and after a few more minutes, she opens her eyes and smiles.

'Welcome home' said Master Owl. Miss Bunny did indeed feel back home again.

'So, tell me more about your experience with Mr Fox' inquired Master Owl.

'He's a builder and mends things' said Miss Bunny, rolling her eyes, 'or at least he would mend things if he actually bothered to turn up! On the rare occasions when he does actually arrive, he always has an excuse.'

'For example, one time he said he was late because he ran into an elephant who wanted her house to be painted pink and it took him ages to find enough pink paint and ladders to do the job! I mean, who has ever seen a pink elephant house!?

Then another time he said he was late because he was accidently mistaken for a large mouse and grabbed by an eagle with bad eyesight, who lifted him up in the air and took him miles away! I mean, who has ever seen an eagle pick up a fox?!

Last time he was late arriving at my house, he told me he had tripped over a blind tortoise, twisted his ankle and fell into a large hole, but somehow, he still managed to walk to me, with no limp. Master Owl, I am not sure Mr Fox is telling the truth!'

Master Owl nodded and smiled, 'I think we should go and pay Mr Fox a visit' he said and off they went in search of this fibbing fox.

On the way through the wood, they ask other animals if they know where Mr Fox lives and each told of their own stories of how he lied to them.

Mr Badger shows them his front door, which fell of its hinges when he opened it. The door crashed to the ground. Miss Bunny decided not to ask Mr Fox to mend her front door after all!

Mrs Mouse complains about Mr Fox and his attempt to mend her door-bell. When Miss Bunny presses the door-bell, a jet of water squirts in her face!

Mr Hedgehog said he had asked Mr Fox to mend her favourite armchair. She invited Miss Bunny to sit on this chair and as she sat down the legs fell off, the back of the chair came lose and she fell on the ground. She tried hard not to laugh, as she could see that Mr Hedgehog was not finding it funny.

Clearly Mr Fox was not only unreliable, but also not very good at mending things. However, it wasn't that he didn't know how to mend things, but he was always in such a rush, that he was slap-dash. He didn't take the time to do the job properly.

One by one, the unhappy animals directed Master Owl and Miss Bunny to the home of Mr Fox.

It is a very sorry looking house.

The front fence is half finished. The gate is half hanging off.

The front door didn't look much better than Miss Bunny's broken door. Some of the windows have broken glass panes. There are also piles of rubbish all over Mr Fox's garden. Miss Bunny thought to herself that if she had seen Mr Fox's own house sooner, she would not have asked him to do anything!

Master Owl presses Mr Fox's doorbell and is relieved to find there is not a jet of water squirting in his face!! In fact, it even made a bell ring inside. After a few moments, the front door opens (more or less) and there stands Mr Fox.

He is wearing overalls, with a pencil appearing

out of the top pocket. His hair is very messy and seems to be sprinkled in sawdust.

'Hello Miss Bunny' said the Fox, 'I was just about to leave and come over to your place to mend your front door, but a beaver had a problem with his parachute and just crashed through my roof. It's taken me ages to mend the hole.'

Miss Bunny ignored that lie and said, 'hello Mr Fox, let me introduce you to my teacher and friend, Master Owl.'

'Hello Mr Fox' said Master Owl, 'I have heard a lot about you today.'

Mr Fox laughed nervously and asked 'good things I hope?'

Miss Bunny had to bite her lip, not to laugh out loud!

'Can we come in and sit down with you' said the wise old owl, 'we would like to show you something.'

The three animals all sit down in Mr Fox's living room. Miss Bunny is relieved when Master Owl suggests they all sit on the floor together. She looked at the chairs and didn't trust them not to fall apart!

'OK Mr Fox, you seem to be very busy, which is why Miss Bunny and I would like to share something with you that we call a Magical Mindful Moment.'

Master Owl asks his friends to close their eyes and take three deep breaths in and out. They settle down into their own bodies. He asks them to notice the feel of their legs touching the rug on the ground. Then he asks them to notice the sounds around them.

At first Mr Fox's mind is spinning with so many thoughts, such as how long this would take because he had lots of animals to see and lots of houses to mend.

But after a short while, the calming voice of Master Owl starts to have a dramatic effect on him. He feels himself relax and settle down. His mind becomes less busy as he takes his attention to his body.

Eventually Mr Fox opens his eyes and looks at his new friends, sitting very peacefully in front of him.

'How do you feel now?' asks Master Owl.

'Wow' replied Mr Fox, 'I can see why you call it a Magical Mindful Moment. I feel so different. What has happened to me?'

'Nothing has really happened' said Master Owl, 'you have just come back home to yourself, that's all. So, my friend, tell me what you feel, in this moment?'

Mr Fox takes some deep breaths and his head drops down, his eyes looking at the ground.

'I have been lying to all the other animals and to myself,' he said, looking like he was about to burst into tears.

'That's good to admit that' said Master Owl, 'but let's find out why you have not been telling the truth. Tell me now how you are feeling inside?'

Mr Fox takes a few more deep breaths and then says, 'I feel sadness that I don't have any friends.'

'You have myself and Miss Bunny as friends now' said Master Owl, reassuringly.

Mr Fox smiles when he hears that.

Master Owl continues. 'Do you feel anything else underneath the sadness?'

After a moment, Mr Fox replied, 'yes, I feel afraid, scared.'

'Scared of what?' asks Miss Bunny sympathetically.

'Scared of the other animals not liking me, so I don't want to let them down and upset them. That's why I have been lying so much, trying to keep everybody happy,' said Mr Fox, looking quite sad.

Master Owl explains that the reason why we tell lies is usually because we are afraid of upsetting others.

He says 'honesty means to tell the truth without any expectations.'

After some quiet moments, Mr Fox spoke. 'Thank you, Master Owl. I don't want to lie to the other animals anymore. It's been making me feel awful telling all these lies. I have been feeling so unhappy inside. What can I do to turn this all around? I have made such a mess of everything.'

'It's very simple' said Master Owl, 'go and re-visit all the animals that you have let down, say sorry and offer to fix their problems for free. Some animals may not want to see you, so just leave a note for them. But others will be pleased to hear your apology.

Then once you have done this, I suggest you go and visit Miss Deer at the Animal Hospital and offer to help look after the buildings for one day a week, again for no charge.'

Mr Fox nods and a little smile creeps across his face. He actually started to look happy for the first time in many years.

It is time for Master Owl and Miss Bunny to leave Mr Fox and return to their Home tree. Miss Bunny hops and Master Owl flies through the trees. Sometimes she flew on his back, but she preferred to stay on the ground.

When they were back home, Miss Bunny had some thoughts to share with her teacher.

'I really feel for Mr Fox. It can be really hard to tell the truth sometimes, because we don't want to hurt people's feelings. I remember when I was younger, my Mother used to make me a carrot pie which I really didn't like, but I was too scared to tell her what I thought, so I had to keep eating it!'

Master Owl said 'so even though you thought you were being kind to your mother, you kept suffering each time you ate the carrot pie?'

'Yes!' said Miss Bunny, 'it tasted yucky!'

'And your poor Mother' said Master Owl, 'only wanted to give you food that was tasty and delicious, but how would she know you didn't like it, if you didn't say anything?'

'Good point' said Miss Bunny 'so how could I have told her the truth?'

'With gratitude' he said. 'You could have said something like this. Dear Mother, I love how you cook for me and look after me. I am really grateful for everything you do, however I am not that keen on your carrot pie. Would you mind if I helped you with the cooking now and again, so I can learn how to cook? Maybe we can create some new yummy dishes of food together?'

'Yes, I can see that was the honest and kind way to talk to my Mother' said Miss Bunny.

Over the next few weeks, Mr Fox follows Master Owl's advice and visits all the animals he had let down. Some didn't even want to see him, but most give him a second chance and this time, he takes his time and does a great job. He makes sure he is mindful while he is mending things, rather than thinking about the next job he was going onto. This made a huge difference to his work.

Mr Fox also worked one day a week at the Animal Hospital. Miss Deer was very grateful for his help. The day he spent at the hospital was the highlight of his week.

Two months later there is a huge storm. A bolt of lightning hits a tree and it falls on Mr Fox's house. It is completely destroyed. He sets about re-building his house, but to Mr Fox's total amazement, all the other animals in the wood offer to help him re-build his house. By helping the other animals and telling the truth, he had discovered a whole new community in the woodland.

He visits Master Owl and Miss Bunny and thanks them for helping him turn around his life. He tells them 'the truth really has set me free!'

Miss Bunny sits with Master Owl, on the usual branch, quietly thinking about Mr Fox. She decides there and then that she will always do her best to tell the truth, no matter what. She wants to be a free as Master Owl. Fluid and free.

She closes her eyes and enjoys the sounds in the wood.

MASTER OWL'S WISE WORDS

Telling the truth can feel so scary sometimes. This is totally natural. We don't like to upset people. But the truth about truth is that people prefer to know how you are REALLY feeling, rather than hearing a lie.

When you tell people the truth, you not only set yourself free, but you also free them too. Let's say you are about to go and visit someone but you don't really enjoy spending time with them, but to be polite you don't say anything. Then you have an unhappy time with them and so do they, if you are not happy.

But if you let them know you don't want to spend time with them, this gives you the freedom to spend more time with people you do actually like AND it gives them time to find new friends that they get on better with. Everybody wins. Truth and honesty win.

Telling lies all the time is very exhausting, as you have to remember what lies you tell to which people. If you are honest, then life is so much easier.

The funny thing is that when you tell a lie to someone, very often people know you are not being honest! They can tell and it can be confusing for them.

I have a saying I like which is: 'Truth is its own reward'. This means that telling the truth makes us feel good inside. But that does not mean you have to unkind to people. There is usually a way to tell the truth in a kind and thoughtful way.

7. ELEPHANT'S BIG LESSON

The first rays of sunlight spread through the wood.

The morning chorus is starting and to no-one's surprise, Master Owl is out sitting on his favourite branch, eyes closed. He is enjoying a Magical Mindful Moment and feeling very peaceful. He loved the aliveness of life.

Meanwhile, Miss Bunny is also up early. She

makes her way quietly up the spiral stairs that run around Master Owl's Home tree.

Up and up she climbs, holding onto some kind of a ruck sack.

She creeps along the branch and slips the bag onto Master Owl's back. He does not seem to notice, but because he was so mindful, he knew exactly what was going on.

He keeps still.

He loves Miss Bunny's little pranks.

After a few minutes, Master Owl looks so relaxed that he falls backwards off his branch and heads down to the ground below.

At that moment, Miss Bunny shouts 'open parachute!' But nothing happened. No parachute. So down he went.

Master Owl lands safely in a pile of leaves. Feathers went in all directions. Some moments later he opens his eyes and speaks, with a twinkle in his eye.

'Good morning Miss Bunny. Why am I wearing

an unopened parachute on my back?!'

'Morning' she said, 'I was hoping it would open up and stop you falling to the ground!'

Master Owl chuckled to himself and said,

'Miss Bunny, you know I am a bird, don't you? This means I know how to fly! I don't need a parachute!'

'Not all birds can fly,' she said, 'like an ostrich – they can't fly.'

'Yes, that's true that not all birds can fly, but owls can!' said Master Owl, as he flew back up to his branch and brushed off the leaves.

'But thank you Miss Bunny for thinking about me. I really appreciate all you do. Why don't you have a go with the parachute? Seeing as rabbits really can't fly! Maybe you can be the first flying bunny?'

Miss Bunny takes the parachute. She climbs up to the very top of the Home tree. But when she reaches the top, she smells smoke.

'That's strange,' she thinks to herself, 'I wonder

what's making that smell?'

As she looks, she sees a plume of smoke in the distance, rising from the forest.

'It's a fire!' She climbs quickly back down to tell Master Owl.

'Hop on Miss Bunny' said Master Owl, 'and leave that parachute behind. Just stick with me. I know how to fly!'

Miss Bunny jumps onto his back and holds on tightly. They fly together, heading for the smoke they can see and smell in the distance.

Once they locate where the smoke is coming from, they land.

Part of the woodland is on fire. It is a shocking sight.

The first thing they see is an enormous elephant, carrying huge trees in his trunk.

'Hello Mr Elephant,' said the owl, 'what's happening here? Why is this part of the forest on fire?'

'Hello owl,' said the elephant gruffly, 'this is

none of your business, so you can leave.'

Miss Bunny whispers in Master Owl's ear 'how rude!' Master Owl smiles and keeps talking with the elephant.

'I live in the forest too Mr Elephant, so does Miss Bunny and so do many other animals, so this is ALL our business,' he said.

'Well,' said Mr Elephant, 'I own this part of the forest and I am clearing all the trees and burning the tree stumps, so I can sell the wood and grow crops. This will make me lots of money!' He said this with a wicked little smile.

He goes back to work, using his trunk to make huge piles of trees that he had cut down.

Miss Bunny looks really upset.

'Master Owl' she said, 'this is awful. Surely he doesn't own part of the forest and even if he did, he is cutting down all these lovely old trees. That's so sad.' She starts to cry.

Master Owl looks thoughtful.

'Miss Bunny,' he said, 'sometimes we have to be

very patient in life and give our fellow animals time to learn the lessons they most need to learn. Come, let us leave now.'

Miss Bunny jumped back onto Master Owl's back. She wiped the tears from her eyes. She trusted her teacher, even though she wants to try and stop Mr Elephant from chopping down any more trees. But she is only a little rabbit, so what could she do to stop a huge, heavy and very determined elephant.

The weeks went by and about a month later, Miss Bunny and Master Owl are sheltering together up in his house from really heavy rain outside. It was not normal rain at all. It was like a huge tap in the sky had been turned on.

Miss Bunny felt a bit safer up in the tree, rather than down in her house in the tree roots. She didn't want to be in her house if it flooded.

Cracks of thunder and lightning raged all around.

'Master Owl,' she said, 'its very unusual all this rain. It's been raining now for over a week. Why is the weather so different from usual?'

'When we change our forest, the weather patterns change too,' he replied.

'Yes, that makes sense,' said Miss Bunny, 'I remember the first lesson you taught me, which is that everything is connected.'

'Yes, my wonderful student, all living things and all events are on a circle. So what happens on one part of the circle affects everything else,' he said.

'Let me give you an example' said the wise owl.

'Go and sit on my old kitchen table and saw off one of the legs while you are sitting on it!'

'Are you sure?' said Miss Bunny, looking very confused.

'Yes' he said.

'OK, well if you are sure,' she said.

Miss Bunny fetched a saw, sat on the old kitchen table and began to saw off one of the four legs!

Not surprisingly, as the leg fell off, the table crashed to the ground and Miss Bunny slid down the table top onto the floor.

'You OK?' Master Owl asked.

'Yes' replied Bunny, 'I think I learnt the lesson. Everything is connected and when we change something, it comes back to effect us.'

'Exactly' said Master Owl. 'Some of us call this 'karma'. It's one of the laws of the Universe. Every action has a consequence.'

At that exact moment there is a large rumble, which is getting louder and louder.

At first they thought it was another clap of thunder, but then it dawned on them that it was coming from down on the ground, not up in the sky.

They peek out of the door. To their great surprise, they first see what looks like the remains of a huge wooden house. It is being washed away in a river of mud. Miss Bunny is very glad the Universe had given her the idea of being up in the tree that day.

As they look on, the noises got even louder and suddenly there is Mr Elephant. He is also being washed away in the mud-slide.

'Quick Miss Bunny,' said the owl, 'grab that rope you use to tie me onto my branch sometimes, we are going to help Mr Elephant.'

Miss Bunny quickly fetches the rope and gives it to Master Owl. He flies down to the very scared elephant and drops one end of the rope down. Mr Elephant catches it with his trunk.

Master Owl then flies round and round a tree with the rest of rope. Then in one dramatic moment, Mr Elephant comes flying out of the mud-slide. He lands in a wet and muddy heap at the feet of Master Owl and Miss Bunny.

Mr Elephant let out a huge blast of relief from his trunk.

'What happened to you?' asks Miss Bunny.

'I don't know,' said the very upset looking elephant. 'One moment I was sheltering from this storm in my house. The next moment, the house collapsed and was washed away in a river of mud. Then I was washed away too. Thank you so much Master Owl for rescuing me. You have just saved my life.'

'You are most welcome, my friend. Come and get yourself cleaned up and we will talk.'

Mr Elephant uses some fresh water from a bucket Miss Bunny had fetched to wash away the mud off his body. Thankfully the rain stops and the sun comes out again. The sunlight felt amazing on the elephant's body and helped him to dry and warm up.

'Mr Elephant' said Master Owl, 'I think we should take a Magical Mindful Moment together.' Mr Elephant looks confused, but because this wonderful owl had saved his life, he didn't say anything.

The three animals all sit down in the sunlight.

Master Owl asks them to close their eyes. He

says to take some deep breaths in and out.

Mr Elephant breathes in slowly through his trunk. He keeps breathing in and breathing in until he has filled his huge lungs with air.

Then he let all that air out. WHOOSH. He accidentally blows Miss Bunny right over onto her back!

Master Owl's feathers flutter in the wind from the elephant's trunk, but he is well grounded. He doesn't move at all.

After a few moments of slow breathing, Mr Elephant began to relax and sink into the leaves on the forest floor.

Master Owl asks them to be aware of the sounds and smells around them.

They could smell the leaves as they dried in the sunlight.

They could hear a distant rumble of thunder as the storm moved away in the far distance.

After some long mindful moments, Mr Elephant suddenly opened his eyes. He had a look of amazement on his face.

'Are you OK?' asks Miss Bunny, worried.

'Yes' he replied, 'I have just realised something.'

'What did you realise?' asked Miss Bunny, really interested. She knew how magical these mindful moments could be.

'I have realised why my house was washed away in that big storm,' said Mr Elephant. 'By cutting down all those trees, there were no roots to hold the soil together. So when the rains came, all the soil was washed away into the river, including the crops I was trying to grow. Followed by my house and then me!'

Miss Bunny looked at Master Owl.

She thought about what happened when she sawed off the table leg of the table she was sitting on. She had created her own problem, just like this poor elephant had when he cut down all those trees.

'Yes, you are right' said Master Owl to the Elephant. 'Shall we go and see what else happened after you took down all those trees?'

This time, Master Owl and Miss Bunny hitched a ride on the back of Mr Elephant. They set off for the part of the forest where all the trees had been removed.

On their way there, they kept bumping into so many animals. They were walking with suitcases and looking very sad.

'What's up with them?' Miss Bunny asked Master Owl.

'They are homeless, because they all lived in and around those trees.'

Mr Elephant couldn't believe what he had done. He shook his head and his big ears flopped left and right.

He didn't mean to make those animals homeless. He simply didn't think it all through. He was so keen to make money.

In that moment, a totally new thought popped into the elephant's head. The idea hit him like a bolt of lightning. He stopped in his tracks. A big smile came over his face.

'I know what I am going to do' he said, 'I am going to plant the trees again and create a nature reserve for the other animals. Then they know it's safe for them to live in this part of the forest again.'

'That's a wonderful idea' said Master Owl.

'I will start building little homes for these animals now, until the trees grow back again' said Mr Elephant.

My work here is done, thought Master Owl to himself. 'Hang on to my back Miss Bunny, time to head back home.'

They said their goodbyes to Mr Elephant. 'Thank you so much you two' said the Elephant, 'I can never thank you enough.'

Miss Bunny climbed on and off they flew back to their Home tree.

When they arrived back, they made some tea and sat together on Master Owl's favourite branch.

'What happened to Mr Elephant?' she asked Master Owl. 'One moment he was cutting down all those trees. Then the next moment he was going to save the forest and plant more trees.'

'Sometimes in life' the wise bird replied, 'we have to be knocked down to the ground to come to our senses.'

'Or swept away in a mud-slide!' added Miss Bunny.

Master Owl nodded, 'yes this is true. You could call it a 'rude awakening.'

So many of us are asleep, in a way. We don't realise that our actions have far reaching effects on our environment. Mr Elephant woke up in one magical moment and he changed. Luckily once you see it, you can't un-see it.'

'Amazing' replied Miss Bunny, 'so in a way he went from seeing life as a straight line, where nothing is connected, to a life where everything is connected, like on a circle?'

'Yes,' he replied. He was so pleased with Miss Bunny. She was really starting to see how all things were joined up and connected together.

MASTER OWL'S WISE WORDS

Sometimes we don't notice how our actions affect other people or other things in the world. We tend to think that what we do is not connected to other events, especially when these things happen far away from us, like on the other side of the world.

Some people call this 'karma', which simply means that every action has a consequence or result. Mr Elephant learned that by cutting down all those trees, that other animals lost their homes and the soil was washed away, meaning nothing could grow anymore.

So how does one person have a positive effect on something as huge as the weather or climate change? We just have to each do something to make a change, like recycle our waste or help clear rubbish from a beach.

This could be called 'The Power of One', because when millions of people all do something to help, the world changes for the better.

What can you do to help the world? Every little thing you do helps. Together we can make a huge difference. And if it all seems too huge, then just take one small step in the right direction.

 The journey of a thousand miles starts with one small step.

 YOU ARE POWERFUL. Please never forget that.

8. THE HOARDING SQUIRREL

There is one animal who never stops working in the autumn months. He is called Mr Squirrel.

The race is on for him to collect up as many acorns as possible. He then stores them, high up in his tree, in a special hiding place.

He is so greedy that when he can't hold any more acorns in his little hands, he stuffs one in each of his cheeks! He looks quite stupid, but he doesn't care.

Mr Squirrel doesn't care what he looks like because he doesn't have any friends anyway. It's fair to say, he is a miserable old squirrel.

'Come on, come on, quickly, quickly,' he mumbles to himself. He works fast to collect up all the acorns before the other animals find them.

Before too long his storage room is brimming with nuts. He can't fit anymore in there. He is a total hoarder.

Mr Squirrel is very, very selfish and he only thinks about himself.

The autumn turned into winter. The first flakes of snow started to fall.

It turned the wood in a magical white wonderland. Mr Squirrel stayed warm and cosy in his tree home, sleeping next door to his massive pile of food. He would not be running out of acorns this winter.

On the other side of the wood, there on a branch, with his eyes closed, covered in snow, sits wise Master Owl.

He loves the peace and silence of the winter. He has so many warm feathers that he never gets cold.

Little flakes of snow land on his head and his beak, but he doesn't move. He is having a Magical Mindful Moment, noticing the gentle sound of the wind moving through the trees. Every now and again he could hear a clump of snow falling off a leaf, when there was too much snow for the leaf to hold it.

His apprentice and friend Miss Bunny is not sitting out in the cold. She is tucked up warm and snug in her little house at the bottom of Master Owl's Home tree. She has a roaring fire going and is drinking a lovely cup of tea, when suddenly she hears a loud THUMP in the snow outside her front door.

She goes outside to see what made the noise.

She is shocked to find Master Owl lying on the ground on his back chuckling to himself! He had been feeling so peaceful on his favourite branch that for once he actually did fall off! He landed in a deep pile of freshly fallen snow.

'Are you OK Master Owl?' asked Miss Bunny, a little worried.

'Hello Miss Bunny. Sorry to disturb you and bring you out into the cold,' he replied.

'That's fine' she said, 'but what are you doing?'

'Snow angels' he said, as he flapped his wings backwards and forwards in the snow!

With his huge wings he made the best snow angel Miss Bunny had ever seen. She jumped in the snow and had a go too, but her little bunny arms only made a very small snow angel. She loved the snow, at least for a short time anyway.

They both started giggling and their laughter filled the quiet wood for a few moments. Then she headed back into the warmth of her little house to get warm again.

Master Owl flew back up to his branch and settled back down for some more peaceful moments.

As the winter wore on, many of the other animals started to run out of food and became really hungry.

They knew that Mr Squirrel had a huge stockpile of food, so they knocked on his door and asked if he could spare any of his acorns.

'Can I have some food please?' asked Mr Hedgehog.

'NO! GO AWAY!' he shouted, rudely.

'Can you spare some nuts please?' asked Mrs Mouse.

'Sorry, I cannot HEAR you!' he shouted back.

'But we are hungry' cried the other animals, 'please can we have some of your food?'

'No you can't. It's my food. You should have collected more food before the winter arrived. Leave me alone!'

Mr Hedgehog, Mrs Mouse and the other animals left, feeling sad, cold and hungry. They really, really didn't like Mr Squirrel. He was the most annoying and selfish animal in the whole wood. No wonder he didn't have any friends.

As the winter months wore on, the snow eventually started to melt and life returned once more to the forest. Beautiful lime green leaves started to open on all the trees. Fresh new flowers started popping up all over the place. Miss Bunny loved the spring time.

One sunny spring morning, Master Owl and Miss Bunny are enjoying a quiet moment together. They are both sitting on Master Owl's favourite branch, although Miss Bunny has made a little seat to sit on.

Master Owl falls off his branch all the time, she thought to herself, maybe he would like me to make him a seat.

As she was thinking this, they were nearly both knocked off the branch as Mr Squirrel came charging past them, muttering under his breath. 'Get out of my way, get out of my way.'

'Who was that?' asked a shocked Miss Bunny.

'That was my old friend Mr Squirrel,' replied Master Owl. 'He hasn't changed. Always in a mad rush collecting up food.'

After a few moments, Mr Squirrel comes back

down the tree towards our mindful heroes. He trips on a little branch and drops his handful of acorns which he had been collecting. All the food fell to the ground.

Mr Squirrel stops and looks like he is about to scream. He glares at Master Owl and Miss Bunny and stops moving all together.

'My dear Mr Squirrel' said Master Owl kindly, 'would you join Miss Bunny and me for a Magical Mindful Moment?'

'I have no idea what that is' replied the worried looking squirrel.

'Let me show you' said Master Owl 'it's really very simple.'

Mr Squirrel sits down on the branch between Miss Bunny and Master Owl. He didn't need a seat, he was very good at climbing trees. Probably the best tree climber in the wood in fact.

'Right' said Master Owl, 'now close your eyes both of you and take a deep breath in . . . and then let it out slowly. And another breath in . . . and out again.'

Mr Squirrel and Miss Bunny felt their bodies relax as they noticed their breath going in and out of their noses.

Mr Squirrel is really quite shocked. He is so busy normally that he hadn't noticed his breathing before.

Master Owl then asks them to notice the feel of the bark under their feet.

He asks them to listen to the noises all around them in the woodland.

Mr Squirrel had never noticed the feel of the

bark under his feet. And he certainly had never noticed the sounds in the wood. This was all a very new experience for him.

Then Master Owl asks his students to notice how they were feeling. Mr Squirrel felt this huge surge of sadness rise up inside him and he started to cry.

Big drops of tears splashed down his cheeks and fell all the way to the ground. Any little animal on the ground might have thought it had started raining.

'Well done Mr Squirrel' said Master Owl gently, 'it's good to notice how we are feeling and, in this case, let the sadness out.'

'I am so sorry Master Owl and Miss Bunny' he said, wiping the tears from his eyes, 'I don't know what has come over me.'

'That's absolutely fine' said Master Owl, 'sometimes we are so busy we forget about our self and we get lost. So, taking a Magical Mindful Moment helps us to find ourselves again, simply by noticing how we are feeling.'

'Well, I didn't know I was feeling so sad' said Mr Squirrel, 'until I literally bumped into you and nearly knocked you both off this branch.'

'I think we were meant to meet today' said Miss Bunny. 'Since I have been a student of Master Owl, I've noticed that things keep happening when you least expect it.'

'Yes Miss Bunny, you are right' said the wise old bird, 'in life we don't always get what we want, but we always get what we need.'

'Mr Squirrel, can you tell us why you feel so sad?' asked Master Owl.

Mr Squirrel went quiet and thought carefully, then said 'yes, I am sad because I don't have any friends.'

'That's sad,' said Miss Bunny. 'Before I met Master Owl I thought I was all alone but he helped me to see that I was connected to all things in the wood. Why don't you have any friends?'

'It's because I don't share any of my food with the other animals, even when they are hungry and desperate,' replied a very sorry looking squirrel.

'And why do you collect and store so many more nuts than you actually need for yourself to live off?' enquired Master Owl.

'That is a really good question,' said Mr Squirrel. 'I have never stopped to think about it before, always been so busy collecting food.'

Master Owl then asks 'did something happen to you when you were little squirrel growing up?'

Mr Squirrel looks confused, scratches his head until this strange look came over him. His eyes open wide. He looks like he has realised something really important.

'Yes' he said 'my family once ran out of food one winter. It was awful. We were so hungry. Is this why I collect nuts like some kind of nutter? Because I am scared?'

'Yes' said Master Owl wisely, 'when we go through difficult times early in our life, it leaves a mark on us. Most of us don't even realise this has affected us. We run on automatic.'

'Wow that's amazing' said Miss Bunny. 'I hadn't realised what an effect our experiences have on us when we are growing up.'

'Yes' said Master Owl, 'so taking time to have a mindful moment can allow magic to happen. It's so helpful when we start to notice what we are feeling and understand why we are feeling like we do.'

'Let's all take a moment to take three nice deep breaths in and out,' said Master Owl quietly.

All three animals close their eyes. They take three lovely long breaths in and out.

'So wise Master Owl' said in a much more relaxed Mr Squirrel, 'how do I overcome my fear of running out of food in the winter?'

'You will need to be brave and trust in life' the owl replied.

'Why?' said Mr Squirrel.

'Because' said Master Owl, 'I would like you to give away almost all your supply of nuts to the other animals in the wood.'

Mr Squirrel didn't move. He looked quite

shocked. All he could say was 'why?'

Master Owl continues, 'because the more you give away, the more you will have.'

Both Mr Squirrel and Miss Bunny look confused about this latest wisdom from Master Owl.

Miss Bunny speaks first, 'but how can you have more of something if you give it away?!'

'Trust me' said Master Owl with a smile, 'but more importantly trust in life. You will see what happens when you give and don't expect anything back.'

After a few quiet moments, Mr Squirrel says he will follow Master Owl's advice. He hopes he is right. He has been so miserable and unhappy. He is willing to try something different.

Off he went, back down the tree, waving to his new friends and thanking them for their help.

When Mr Squirrel returns home to his own tree, he goes up to the place where he stores his nuts and can't believe how much food he has been sitting on. He actually feels quite embarrassed.

Before meeting Master Owl and Miss Bunny he hadn't noticed how much food he had been collecting. He hadn't known why he was collecting so much food. But now he knew why, he trusted Master Owl. One by one he starts to throw the nuts out of his tree. It was soon raining nuts!

He then made a sign up and stuck it on the tree down by the ground. It read:

'Free nuts – please help yourself'

At first the other animals didn't believe Mr Squirrel with his offer of free food. They thought about him hoarding all those nuts and weren't sure whether to trust his offer.

Mr Hedgehog decides to be brave and starts talking with Mr Squirrel. Almost straightaway he realises there is something different about Mr Squirrel. He is calmer and nicer. A lot less silly, that's for sure! Mr Hedgehog collects a handful of nuts, saying thank you and heads home.

Mrs Mouse sees Mr Hedgehog walking away with handfuls of nuts and also goes to say hello to the squirrel. She only has little hands, but she gratefully takes one large round delicious acorn, says thank you and walks back to her little house. She turns and looks at Mr Squirrel as she walks away. He has a lovely happy smile on his face.

She had never seen him smile before.

After a few days, the enormous pile of nuts that had been sitting at the bottom of the tree was completely gone. Mr Squirrel takes down the sign and climbs back up to his house, high up in the tree.

Much time passed.

The summer turned into autumn.

The autumn turned into winter. It snowed again, covering the whole wood in a beautiful white soft blanket of snow.

Mr Squirrel's supply of food is getting smaller and smaller until one cold miserable day he completely runs out of food.

But the word went out around the wood that Mr

Squirrel had run out of food and something truly remarkable happens.

The animals, who had collected nuts back in the spring, start to bring some of this food back. They leave it in a little pile at the bottom of Mr Squirrel's tree. Mr Hedgehog brings round five acorns. Mrs Mouse brings round all she could carry in her little hands – one juicy acorn.

When Mr Squirrel starts to see this happen, he can't believe his eyes. The other animals are bringing HIM food!

These animals were so grateful for the food that he shared with them earlier in the year. All they wanted to do was help him out in his time of need.

He is so grateful to the other animals and says THANK YOU every time they drop off some acorns at the bottom of his tree.

With the support of his woodland community, Mr Squirrel is able to survive the winter and he learns a valuable lesson he would never, ever forget.

When he gave away all of those nuts, he might have had less food but he gained so much more, in so many ways that he could ever have imagined.

He discovered kindness and friendship. He discovered a sense of community amongst the other animals that lived with him in the wood.

Mr Squirrel realises he is not alone anymore. He is an important part of the community and he feels so different about his life.

He is not afraid anymore.

And when the spring came around again, he helps teach the other animals how to collect up nuts. He shows them how to store the acorns safely, so that everybody has enough food to last the winter.

Back at Master Owl's Home tree, Miss Bunny hears all about Mr Squirrel and what had happened to him over that previous winter.

'Master Owl' she said, 'now I understand what you meant when you said that the more you give away, the more you have.

It didn't make any sense to me at the time, but it makes so much sense now.'

Master Owl smiled and said 'yes when we give, we find that life gives us so much back, in so many unexpected ways. All we have to do is remember to be kind, to be generous and trust.'

'And remember not to fall off your branch while having a Magical Mindful Moment!' jokes Miss Bunny with a big smile.

Master Owl laughed. He loved Miss Bunny's little jokes.

They both sat silently together on their favourite branch, enjoying the feeling of the warm spring sun on their bodies.

MASTER OWL'S WISE WORDS

Giving always does so much good. I like to say: 'Give and give without a care and watch for wonders everywhere!'

When we give without any expectations, it feels good in our heart. In fact, it's one way we know that we are all connected together, because in helping others, we help ourselves too. It's like we are joined together in an enormous circle!

Mr Squirrel gained so much by being generous, even if it seemed a strange thing to do at the time.

When we think just about ourselves, we can sometimes feel unhappy. But when we think about other people and do something kind to help them, it makes us feel happy. So, if you are ever feeling unhappy, just volunteer to help someone in your family, your school or local community. I promise you will feel happier in no time.

That's a Master Owl top tip!

9. THE MISERABLE MOUSE

It is just before dawn and Master Owl is already out on his favourite branch. He loves watching the sunrise and hearing the start of the birds morning chorus. Ever so gently the clouds start to turn pink as the sun once again rolls up and brings light, warmth and life to all living things.

He closes his eyes and sits peacefully, being aware of the sounds and sensations around him.

Miss Bunny never really realises just how aware Master Owl is!

She creeps along the branch and gently ties his feet to the branch, hoping that he wouldn't notice. She didn't like Master Owl falling off his branch and it was their little joke – she was always trying to stop him from falling off.

Master Owl pretends he had not heard Miss Bunny. With his eyes still closed, he allows himself to fall backwards off the branch, but the rope was so tight that he just hung upside down!

He opens one eye and says out loud, 'am I bat now? I seem to be upside down!' There is an actual bat, hanging upside down beside him, who looks at him with a confused look. Probably never seen a bat as large as Master Owl!

Then he starts chuckling to himself. 'Miss Bunny' he said, 'have you tied my feet to the branch?'

'Yes,' she replied, 'sorry, I didn't mean to change you into a giant feathered bat!'

'That's OK,' he said with a smile. 'I forgive you, but can you please untie me now so that we can have breakfast?'

Miss Bunny pushes him back around so he is the right way up and unties the ropes.

They sit together and eat their breakfast.

'Thank you for forgiving me' said Miss Bunny.

'You are welcome, but really there is nothing to forgive,' said Master Owl.

Miss Bunny went quiet for a while and then a troubled look appeared on her face.

'I don't think I have forgiven my Mother for not speaking to me for the last year. We had an argument and had no contact since then,' she said.

Master Owl asked, 'that must be difficult for you, I am sorry. How does it feel to not forgive your Mother?'

'Like a pain in my chest,' she replies. 'I don't like this feeling Master Owl. Is there something I can do about it?'

Just at that moment, the tree starts to shake and all the tea spills out of their cups. Miss Bunny thinks it must be an earthquake, but when she looks down at the ground, it was clearly not an earthquake – it was an enormous elephant!

The Elephant looks up at the tree. She reaches up with her long trunk to where our mindful heroes were having breakfast and says, 'would you like to slide down my trunk to the ground?!'

Miss Bunny and Master Owl look at each other, a little surprised and then both smiled.

They jump onto the trunk and slide down in two smooth movements. Firstly, they ended up looking directly into the elephant's eyes. Secondly, the elephant lowers her trunk to the ground and they slid gently down to the forest floor.

'Thank you!' said Miss Bunny, with a big smile on her face. 'That was the coolest way to come down the tree. I love slides!!'

Miss Bunny was still a little bunny at heart.

Master Owl also loved the slide down the elephant's trunk, but he just smiled quietly to himself.

'Hello Mrs Elephant,' said Master Owl, 'thank you for the lift. Have you met my good friend Miss

Bunny?'

'Good to meet you' said Miss Bunny, still smiling from the slide ride. 'What brings you to this part of the wood?'

'Good day to you both' said Mrs Elephant.

There was a noticeable sadness in her voice. 'To be honest, I have been unhappy for the last two years. This morning when I woke up, all I could think about was going to find this wise owl that so many other animals talk about. I need to ask you for some advice.'

'I am here for you' said Master Owl. 'Do please tell me your story.'

Mrs Elephant started to talk.

'Two years ago, I was minding my own business, just walking in the wood when I accidentally stepped on a mouse's tail. Because I am so heavy, part of her tail broke off and never grew back. This poor mouse has been so miserable ever since.

Of course, I didn't mean to step on her tail, but I am scared of mice and I panicked.

I feel so guilty and it's making me miserable. Would you be able to help me? She won't see me. This has gone on for two years now, but this morning I just felt myself walking to find you, so I hope you can help me.'

'Guilt is a very painful emotion' said Master Owl. 'It's like very sticky glue and can be hard to let go of. I feel for you Mrs Elephant.'

'Yes, you are right, I do feel guilty for hurting this little mouse. But what can be done?' asked Mrs Elephant.

'Come on Miss Bunny,' said Master Owl, 'let's go and see this little mouse and see what we can do to help.'

The three animals set off in search of this miserable mouse. Mrs Elephant moves quickly through the wood, with her huge legs, making the ground shake as she goes.

Miss Bunny takes a ride on Master Owl's back. She loves it when he gives her a lift. Rabbits are not designed to fly, so this is always a special moment for her. To see the trees below her. To see the views of the mountains beyond the wood.

After a little while, Mrs Elephant stops. Master Owl flies down to the ground and Miss Bunny jumps off. They find themselves opposite a sad looking little house. All the curtains are shut, which was strange for the middle of the day.

Master Owl knocks gently on the front door.

There is no reply, so he turns the door handle. It was not locked, so he opens the door.

He and Miss Bunny bend down and walk in through the little door. Mrs Elephant waits patiently outside. There was no way she was going to fit through this little door and she knew what would happen if she tried!

She already felt guilty enough about the mouse's tail, without breaking her little house in a thousand pieces.

Master Owl said 'Twit - ta - hello, anyone there?'

In the darkness and in the gloom, they saw a really miserable looking little mouse.

'Hello Mrs Mouse,' said Master Owl. 'It's a bit dark in here, shall we open the curtains for you?'

'You can if you like,' she said, sounding very unhappy.

Miss Bunny opens the curtains. The sunlight comes streaming through the little windows. There was so much dust, which was now lit by the bright sunlight.

Mrs Mouse didn't look like she had cleaned her little house for many years.

As the light improved, they could see that Mrs Mouse was indeed missing most of a tail. Just a little stump was left, topped off with a bandage.

'So Mrs Mouse, can you tell us what happened to you?'

'Yes, I suppose so,' she said gloomily. 'I was out in the forest one day when this huge, stupid, thoughtless elephant ran past me and stood on my tail. Now look, I just have this little stump of a tail.'

'I am sorry this happened to you' said Miss Bunny, kindly, 'but if you don't mind me asking, why are you still so sad about this when it happened two years ago?'

'I am so angry with that stupid elephant. I will NEVER, EVER forgive her for treading on my tail!' she said.

Master Owl looked thoughtful and then said, 'I am very sorry that you feel this way, because I can see you are suffering greatly from this event. Even though it happened two years ago, it's like it happened today.'

Mrs Mouse nods her head in agreement.

Master Owl continues, 'would you like to be free from your suffering?'

Mrs Mouse looks up at Master Owl, with her eyes wide open and replies, 'yes, but how would that be possible?'

'Can you please come and join me outside' said Master Owl, 'we will take this mindfully.'

Mrs Mouse looks very confused but she gets off her rocking chair. She follows Master Owl and Miss Bunny outside. She has a big shock when she sees the elephant that she hates so much.

She is just about to say something nasty to Mrs Elephant, when Master Owl says 'let's have some silence please.

I am happy to help you both, but we need some silence. Talking will only keep the drama roundabout going around and around.'

All four animals sit down on some comfy leaves. It's a very odd sight, seeing a mouse, an elephant, a rabbit and an owl all sitting in a circle together!

Master Owl asks them all to close their eyes and take some deep breaths in and out. He asks them to feel themselves relax and sink into the leaves. It was time for a Magical Mindful Moment.

He asks them to notice all the sounds around them. The forest was always full of different sounds, but a busy mind does not hear these sounds.

Next he asks them to notice how their bodies were in contact with the ground, to feel the softness of the leaves.

Master Owl knew that mindfulness helps to give us a little 'thinking holiday', as he liked call it.

After a short while, both Mrs Mouse and Mrs Elephant started to feel more relaxed.

Mrs Mouse hears the sound of a woodpecker in the distance, echoing through the trees.

Rat a tat tat.

Rat a tat tat.

Mrs Elephant hears the cooing of a dove, as it sang to another dove.

Coo. Coo. Coo.

Coo. Coo. Coo.

They had never noticed how alive the forest was.

They had been so busy thinking. So busy telling themselves stories about what they THINK had happened to them.

Then without warning, Mrs Mouse bursts into tears and sobs.

Miss Bunny goes and gives her a silent hug.

She knew that when the tears came, this was all part of the mindful moment working its magic. She knew from her own experience that keeping any emotion trapped inside can be painful. It's a bit like a fizzy drink trying to get out of a bottle when the top is still on.

She had learnt from her wise teacher that emotions were actually just energy in motion: e-motion. When we try to stop the energy from moving through us and push it back down, it can cause all sorts of problems.

Miss Bunny is glad to see Mrs Mouse letting the sadness go with her tears.

When Mrs Mouse stops crying, a very small smile started to break across her face. Master Owl and Miss Bunny knew what was going to happen next. They always knew.

Master Owl asks her what thought caused her to smile the first smile she had smiled, in two long miserable years.

'I feel so much better for that cry' she said, wiping away her tears.

'As I sat there quietly listening to the sounds in the forest, I suddenly realised that I was making MYSELF unhappy by not forgiving Mrs Elephant for what was probably just an unfortunate accident.

I have spent every awake minute in the last two years, stuck in that moment and been unable to move on.'

Mrs Elephant couldn't stay quiet any longer and said 'yes, I am so sorry Mrs Mouse. I really didn't mean to step on your tail. To be honest, I am terrified of mice! I panicked when I saw you. I am so sorry. Please forgive me.'

Mrs Mouse's smile got wider and wider.

'Oh Master Owl,' she said, 'by not forgiving Mrs Elephant I was making myself so unhappy. Just staying inside my house with the curtains closed. When I came outside into the light and listened to the sounds in the woods, I came back to this present moment with you and Miss Bunny. Thank you!'

Master Owl smiles and says, 'you are most

welcome. Sometimes all we need to do is to sit quietly and have a little thinking holiday.

Thoughts are just stories we tell ourselves.

In truth, things happen to us, but it's the stories we tell about these things that create the suffering.

Life is full of pleasure and sometimes pain, but suffering is a choice that we don't have to make.'

The animals all took some time to take in what Master Owl had just said.

Then Mrs Mouse went over to speak to Mrs Elephant. 'I realise now that you didn't mean to step on my tail, did you?'

'No, not at all' said a relieved looking elephant. 'I have been feeling so guilty about hurting your tail. It's been eating me up inside for the last two years.'

'And I have also been suffering for the last two years, by blaming you, when it was actually just an accident. I totally forgive you' said Mrs Mouse.

'Thank you so much,' she said, 'that means so much to me. I also forgive myself now for hurting you.'

Mrs Elephant felt this huge weight of guilt leaving her body. Even though she was still a heavy animal, she felt so much lighter. She hadn't felt this happy for years.

Mrs Mouse went to hug the elephant's gigantic leg, but Mrs Elephant looked nervous again.

'Sorry' she said, 'I am still a bit scared of mice.'

Mrs Mouse said, 'how about I come and spend some time with you, so that you overcome your fear of mice? After all I am so much smaller than you, it is me that should be more afraid of you!'

'Yes please' said Mrs Elephant smiling, 'I don't want to suffer from this fear anymore. I don't want to waste another moment of my life!'

Mrs Mouse and Mrs Elephant went off into the woods, as new friends.

She shouts back to Master Owl and Miss Bunny, 'thank you, my wise friend, now I feel FREE!!!' She does a little dance.

Miss Bunny jumps onto Master Owl's back and

they fly back to their Home tree to finish their breakfast.

'So Miss Bunny, what did you learn today?'

'Well,' she replied, 'I saw how very sad Mrs Mouse was by not forgiving Mrs Elephant. She lived for two years in that dark little house, with no light coming in. How awful. But once she realised it was just an accident and that Mrs Elephant was scared of mice, she forgave her! Her smile came back. That really was a Magical Mindful Moment!'

'Yes' said Master Owl, 'there is no peace without forgiveness. It's one of the best gifts you can give yourself.'

Master Owl pauses and then asks, 'and how do you feel now about your Mother not speaking with you for the last year?'

She smiles and replies, 'yes I have completely forgiven her. I can see now she is doing her best and so am I. It's almost certainly just a misunderstanding. I am going to see her tomorrow and give her a big hug. Life is too short not to hold the people you love.

Thank you Master Owl. I feel so much lighter now. In fact, I feel so light, I think I might float up off this branch like a balloon!'

'Perhaps I should tie some rope to your legs for a change, just to stop you floating away' joked Master Owl and they both started laughing.

MASTER OWL'S WISE WORDS

Beliefs are very powerful things. What we believe to be true can be the difference between living a happy and an unhappy life. Mindfulness can give us a quiet space to think about our beliefs and question them.

Mrs Mouse believed that Mrs Elephant has stood on her tail on purpose, to hurt her. This made Mrs Mouse feel very sad and angry. In those two years of living in her dark little house, she never once stopped and asked herself a really important question. Was it true? Was it true that Mrs Elephant was trying to hurt her? Thankfully Mrs Mouse discovered this was not the truth. Mrs Elephant was just terrified of mice and panicked. It was just an accident.

As another wise teacher once said 'the truth will set you free.'

Forgiveness can also set you and others free. Forgiveness is very powerful.

 The strange thing about not forgiving others, is that we are the ones who suffer. When we are angry at others, we are the ones who suffer.

Mrs Mouse and Mrs Elephant both found freedom from suffering. All they had to do was stop, have a mindful moment and question whether what they believed was actually true.

10. Miss Bunny Meets the Dolphins

It is a beautiful summers evening in the woods where Master Owl and Miss Bunny live.

About an hour from sunset, the whole of the wood is filled with golden light filtering through the leaves in the most beautiful way.

Master Owl calls this 'The Golden Hour'.

It is one of his favourite times of day. He felt as if EVERYTHING was made of this Golden Light.

When he was sitting on his branch and having a Magical Mindful Moment, he would often just look around him and be totally amazed by the intelligence of this Golden Light.

Nature was so clever.

The leaves always knew when to fall off in the autumn and grow again in the spring.

The trees always knew how to grow tall and strong by pushing their roots down into the ground.

The flowers always followed the sun's movement throughout the day.

Caterpillars just seemed to know how to build a cocoon and turn into beautiful butterflies.

Birds knew how to build incredible nests, at just the right time before an egg needed a place to be kept warm.

Salmon knew how to swim thousands of miles through the sea and up rivers to reach the exact right spot to lay their eggs.

There was just this beautiful intelligence silently

running the show.

Since meeting Master Owl, Miss Bunny had begun to notice this beautiful intelligence at work in the woods around her. Before she had met this wise old bird, she had never really paid any attention to the life around her. Now she noticed everything.

Master Owl joined Miss Bunny for supper, down in Miss Bunny's little house. This was located in the roots of Master Owl's Home tree.

On the menu tonight is carrot pie, which has a beautiful crusty pastry top. Miss Bunny has cut out a small piece of pastry to look like a carrot. This makes Master Owl smile. He also notices everything.

They are just about to start eating when Miss Bunny asks Master Owl, 'could you please pass me the salt?'

Master Owl hands Miss Bunny the salt shaker.

'Thank you,' she says.

Miss Bunny stops and looks at the salt shaker in

a strange way.

'Are you okay?' asked Master Owl.

'Yes, I'm fine,' said Miss Bunny, 'but I just had the strangest thought. Where does salt come from?'

'That is a brilliant question,' replied Master Owl.

He takes the salt shaker and tips a little bit of salt out on his wing and tastes it.

'This is sea salt,' he said.

'Sea salt,' said Miss Bunny, looking confused. 'What is sea and why does it have salt in it?'

'I'm sorry,' said Master Owl, looking slightly shocked. 'You've never heard of the sea?'

'No,' replied Miss Bunny. 'What is the sea?'

'It's the largest lake of water you've ever seen in your whole life Miss Bunny!' said Master Owl smiling.

'In fact, 70% of this planet is covered in seawater.'

Miss Bunny looks stunned. She had never left

the wood before, so the most water she had seen was a small pond and a stream.

'How far away is the sea?' asked Miss Bunny.

'It would take a couple of hours for me to fly there,' said Master Owl.

He looks at Miss Bunny's face. She is gazing off into the distance, trying to imagine what the sea might look like.

'I think it's time for an adventure to the seaside! Would you like to join me Miss Bunny?'

'Oh yes!' said Miss Bunny excitedly. 'That would be amazing. Can we go right now?'

Master Owl laughed and said, 'let's eat your carrot pie first and get a good night's sleep. We can then head off in the morning.'

Miss Bunny is so excited that she doesn't manage to eat much of her carrot pie. She doesn't manage to sleep that much either.

But when she is sleeping, she keeps dreaming about some very strange animals that she had never seen before. They are like really big fish and they swim very fast. But they seem to be breathing air, just like she did.

She briefly woke up and thought to herself that dreams can be so weird. 'There can't be any animals that breathe air and live in the water. That would be crazy!' Then she falls back deeply asleep.

Little did Miss Bunny know what adventures were waiting for her over the coming days.

Morning eventually arrives and it is a stunning sunrise. The sky is a beautiful deep pink colour. Miss Bunny hopes it is a good sign for their day to come.

She packs up a few belongings in a small bag. A few carrots for the journey. A little blanket to keep her warm at night. Master Owl never got cold at night because he had so many feathers.

'Good morning Miss Bunny,' said Master Owl, 'how did you sleep?'

'Not very well' she replied. 'I was too excited about going to see the sea today. I had these really weird dreams about strange animals that lived in the sea. They breathed air! How crazy!'

Master Owl smiled. He knew that sometimes dreams were messages about something that was going to happen. He knew that time didn't work the way most people thought it did. He was a very clever owl.

'OK Miss Bunny, if you are ready, do you want to hop on my back? We will start our journey. We are going to find out where the salt comes from!'

'Hooray!' said Miss Bunny. She hadn't felt this excited since Christmas morning.

Miss Bunny jumps onto Master Owl's back. They lift up into the sky, climbing up through the trees, higher and higher. Soon they are above all of the trees in the wood.

Miss Bunny never grew tired of the incredible view from the back of her teacher.

With the sun behind them, they head west over the forest. His huge wings beating in a perfect rhythm. Miss Bunny loved the feeling of the wind against her fur.

After nearly two hours of flying, Miss Bunny notices that the landscape is slowly changing underneath them.

She looks down. There are no trees anymore and the colour of the ground was different. It is getting more and more sandy. Some of the sand has started to pile up into little hills.

Miss Bunny is just wondering what these little hills are when Master Owl says, 'we are nearly there Miss Bunny. Look, we have reached the sand dunes.'

'Oh' said Miss Bunny, 'that's what they are, sand dunes.'

'Look ahead,' said Master Owl, with some excitement in his voice.

'Can you see what is coming up?' he asked.

Miss Bunny had been so busy looking at the sand dunes right down below her, she hadn't noticed what was coming up in front of them.

She lifts her head up.

She could not believe the sight that she saw

stretching out in front of her.

There was a huge expanse of water, spreading out as far as the eye could see.

At first, she was so speechless she didn't say a word.

She was having her own Magical Mindful Moment at that point, just taking in the enormity and size of the ocean. It was like her mind had stopped thinking altogether for a few moments.

'Good gracious,' said Miss Bunny, once she had regained her composure. 'Is that the sea?'

'Yes' said Master Owl, 'that's just the very start of it.'

'Get ready for landing, it's time for us to arrive at the beach.'

Master Owl gracefully glides down onto a beautiful sandy beach. It was another perfect landing.

Miss Bunny is quite happy to get off Master Owl's back. It was very comfy being on all those feathers. But she still had to concentrate and hold on tight to make sure she didn't fall off. It's not natural for a bunny to fly, so she was always very happy to be back on the ground.

Miss Bunny just couldn't get over the feel of the sand and the sparkling light on the sea.

She finds her toes digging into the sand. She'd never felt that before. She loves making her feet disappear under the sand and then reappearing again.

She starts giggling.

'Oh Master Owl,' she said, 'thank you so much for bringing me to the beach. I never knew a place like this existed. Up until today I spent all of my life in the wood. I don't know what to say.'

'You're very welcome, my dear friend,' said Master Owl, with a huge smile on his face.

'The ocean is a very special place. I am so happy to be sharing it with you today. Would you like to go and touch the sea now?'

'Yes please!' said Miss Bunny, so excited.

They both walk down the beach towards the

waves that were gently lapping on the shore. Miss Bunny didn't realise how far up the beach a wave would come! She suddenly found her feet all covered in seawater.

'Oh' she said, 'I love the feel of the water on my little feet!'

She put her hand down into the water and pulled it up towards her mouth. She tasted salt.

'Now you know where the salt comes from!' Master Owl winked at her.

'Right Miss Bunny, shall we take a moment now? A special Magical Mindful Moment?'

'Oh yes please,' said Miss Bunny, 'I would love that. It was a very long trip to get here, so I would love to have a mindful moment with you.'

'Yes,' he replied, 'when we have been travelling, it is a really good idea to take some time to rest. We can then fully arrive in the here and now.'

'OK,' Master Owl said, 'let us begin by sitting on the sand and closing our eyes.'

Miss Bunny knew all about mindful moments

but she loved it when Master Owl guided her.

He continued, 'so Miss Bunny, let us take in a lovely deep breath in and out.

In .... and .... out.

In .... and .... out.

In .... and .... out.

Can you feel your belly rising up and falling back?'

Miss Bunny felt so relaxed and peaceful.

He said, 'can you feel the sand beneath your legs and your feet? Just take a moment to notice the sand.'

Miss Bunny loves the feel of the sand on her feet. It feels so warm and comforting to be sitting on the sand. Her mind starts to wonder about whether she would ever really want to go back to the wood. She loves the beach so much.

Master Owl then said, 'now can you hear the sounds around you? Can you hear the sounds of the waves moving up and down the beach?'

Miss Bunny listens to the beautiful rhythm of the waves flowing up onto the sand and then bubbling gently back into the sea again.

She thought to herself that it sounded like the sea was breathing too.

Each wave was like a breath going in and out for the sea. It was one of the most beautiful sounds she'd ever heard.

Master Owl and Miss Bunny just sit for a while, with their eyes closed, listening to the sound of the sea breathing, in and out.

Miss Bunny could have spent the rest of her day just listening to the waves gently lapping on the beach, but she hears a very strange sound.

It was like a WHOOSH of air. But it wasn't just air. It sounded like air and water mixed together.

WHOOSH went the sound again.

She has to open her eyes to see what is making the sound.

To her complete amazement, she sees a strange looking animal in the sea. It is just the same as the animals she saw in her dream the night before. It looks like a huge fish, but it keeps coming up to the surface of the water and making this loud WHOOSH sound. Then it disappears under the surface again for a few seconds and then back out again. Up and down, up and down.

'Master Owl,' she asked, 'what on earth is that animal called? I saw it in my dreams last night, but never thought it was actually a real animal!'

Master Owl smiles and says 'it's called a dolphin.'

'I have never heard of a dolphin before,' said Miss Bunny, looking confused. 'It's the biggest fish I have ever seen and it makes the strangest of whooshing sounds!'

'Dolphins are not actually fish' said Master Owl with a little grin. 'They are air breathing animals, just like you and me.'

'Is that what the whoosh sound is' said Miss Bunny, 'the sound of the dolphin breathing?'

'Yes,' said Master Owl.

'But why don't they breathe through their mouths, like we do?'

'Good question Miss Bunny' said Master Owl. 'They use their mouths for talking and eating fish, but they have a special nose on the top of their heads called a blowhole.'

'Oh, I see' said Miss Bunny, 'so each time they come up to the surface of the water, they take a breath in and out?'

'Actually, they let the breath out and then in, but yes you are right. That whoosh sound is the dolphin making sure all the water has gone from the top of it's blowhole, before taking a breath in. Just like you and me, they don't want water in their lungs.'

'Wow' said Miss Bunny, 'that's so clever that they have a special nose on their heads! How did they end up with a head-nose?!' Miss Bunny starts laughing.

'Dolphins have a head-nose, as you call it, because all of nature is very, very clever,' said Master Owl.

They both just watch the dolphin, gliding in and out of the water. Miss Bunny thinks it is the most beautiful motion she has ever seen an animal doing.

Effortless.

Slippery.

Graceful.

After a short while more silver fins appear in the water and before long there are seven or eight more dolphins. Silently looping in and out of the water. The only noise being the whoosh of the air in and out of their blowholes.

Miss Bunny notices something funny about the dolphins. 'What are they doing in those waves?' she asks.

'The dolphins are surfing' replies Master Owl. 'They are playing and having fun.'

Miss Bunny was stunned. 'I have never seen another animal, just playing. All the animals I know in the wood are busy surviving and collecting food.'

Master Owl smiles, 'yes, we can learn a lot from the dolphins. Shall we go and talk with them?'

'I would love to' said Miss Bunny, 'but I don't know how to swim! I don't have a head-nose!' She looked worried.

'Don't worry my furry friend,' he said, 'I know a much better way of getting out on the sea and we won't get wet.'

Master Owl had large eyes for a good reason. They helped him to have amazing night vision, but they also helped him to see things far away. He had noticed the shell of a huge turtle, bobbing in the sea. It was a little way away from where the dolphins were playing.

'Mr Turtle!' he shouts loudly, 'would you come and give me and Miss Bunny a lift out to the dolphins please?'

Mr Turtle lifts his head up above the water. His eyes narrow and he looks carefully with his small eyes to see who shouted at him. He smiles when he sees his old friend Master Owl standing on the beach, with a very small rabbit next to him.

'Do you know ALL the animals?' asks Miss Bunny.

'Most of them,' said Master Owl laughing.

A few moments later Mr Turtle plods slowly up the beach towards them and says, 'hello my old feathered friend, it's been many years since we last met.'

'Hello Mr Turtle,' said Master Owl, it's wonderful to see you again. This is my very good friend Miss Bunny.'

'Hello,' said Mr Turtle, 'it's lovely to meet you.'

'Hello,' she said, 'I have never met a turtle before. In fact, this is my first time to the beach and seeing the sea.'

'Wow,' said Mr Turtle, 'you've never seen the sea before?'

'I never even knew it existed, until yesterday,' laughed Miss Bunny, 'and here I am today seeing dolphins and turtles. It's amazing!'

Master Owl asks the turtle, 'would you be able to give me and Miss Bunny a lift out on your shell?

We would like to go and talk with the dolphins?'

'Yes of course,' said the big turtle, 'hop on!'

Master Owl and Miss Bunny clamber onto the back of Mr Turtle's huge shell. Once they are sitting down, he plods slowly back into the waves and starts swimming towards the dolphins.

Miss Bunny is a little bit scared as the water laps around her little paws, but she trusts Master Owl. She had never been on a boat before, let alone an alive boat!

After a few minutes they reach the dolphins.

They all pop their heads out of the water and cannot quite believe what they see! It is fair to say that the dolphins had never seen an owl and a rabbit standing on a turtle shell!

'Hello Master Owl' said one of the dolphins, 'we haven't seen you for years! Where have you been hiding?!'

Master Owl smiled and replied 'I have been in the woods, enjoying the beauty of the trees. This is my good friend Miss Bunny. This is her first time to the sea.'

As soon as he said this, all the dolphins swam over and formed a circle around the turtle. They are very curious to see this strange sight.

The dolphins all bob up and down excitedly, blowing air out of the head-noses, as Miss Bunny calls them.

'Hello Miss Bunny' one of the dolphins said, 'how come you never saw the sea before?'

'How can I see something that I didn't even know existed!' she said. 'It's because of the salt on my table at home that I am here today, talking with dolphins on a turtle boat!'

The dolphins looked a bit confused about her 'salt on table' comment, but carried on, 'well, now you have seen the sea, what do you think?'

'It's incredible' she replied, 'I cannot get over how big the sea is!'

The dolphins all started laughing and the one talking said 'the sea is never ending. We have swum in the sea all our lives and we keep discovering new places and making new friends.'

Miss Bunny went quiet for a few moments, as she was thinking of a question to ask them. Then she asked 'what do dolphins do?'

All the dolphins stop, look at each other and then burst out laughing!! They are laughing so hard, they start making waves that come towards the turtle. Miss Bunny looks a little worried, as the turtle moves up and down in the laughter waves, but she is safe.

Once the dolphins stop laughing, the talkative one said 'I am sorry Miss Bunny, we are not laughing at you, it's just your question is so funny.'

'Why is it so funny?' she said, looking a bit confused.

'Because,' the dolphin replied, 'we don't do anything, we just play! Shall we show you some of our favourite games?'

'Yes please,' said Miss Bunny, 'that would be amazing.'

The dolphin continued, 'well, you have already

seen how much we love to surf the waves. That is my favourite thing to do. We wait out back and feel the wave starting to form. Then as it gets higher and higher, we burst out of the wave!'

'How do waves form?' asked Miss Bunny.

'Because the land rises up towards the beach' said the dolphin 'it pushes the water up in a big bump, until the wave crashes down. It goes from a green colour to foaming white water. We have to be careful not to get into the white water and be washed up on the beach.'

'What happens if you get washed up on the beach? Do you have legs?!' she asked.

The dolphins all laughed again. 'No we don't have legs, so we have to be careful not to end up on the beach. We play safely in the waves. The sea is very powerful, so we are always careful when we play.'

'What other games do you like playing' asked a very curious Miss Bunny.

The dolphin replied, 'we all love playing a game

we simply call 'Bubbles.' When we are swimming under water, we can make a ring of bubbles using our blowholes. We then have a competition to see who can swim through the bubble hoop without breaking the circle!'

'Wow,' said Miss Bunny, amazed, 'that sounds so fun. I wish I could play Bubbles with you!'

'I don't think rabbits are very good at swimming under water' said the dolphin, 'so probably best to stay on the turtles shell.'

'Yes, I agree,' said Miss Bunny, looking down at the water and wondering when they would be able to go back to the beach.

Master Owl noticed Miss Bunny looking a bit nervous, so decided it was time to head back to the beach.

'My dear dolphins, we are going to head back to the beach now, but we will see you again soon' he said.

'Thank you for coming to talk with us' said Miss Bunny, 'I have learned so much today already.'

'Come and see us again. Bye bye' said the dolphin. All the dolphins took a deep breath and swam off under the water.

Mr Turtle paddles back to the beach and waddles slowly up onto the dry sand. Master Owl and Miss Bunny hop off. Miss Bunny is very happy to be back on dry land!

'Thank you, Mr Turtle,' said Master Owl, 'you are so kind to give us a lift to meet the dolphins today.'

'You are most welcome,' said the turtle, 'this is the first time I have been a boat for an owl and a rabbit!'

'Goodbye you two' he said and plods slowly back down into the sea.

Miss Bunny watches him enter the water, take a big breath and then dive under the sea. Today she had met two animals who breathed air and lived in the sea. She was quite sure that rabbits were not designed to live in the sea. She preferred the land, that was for sure.

'So, my dear Miss Bunny' said Master Owl, 'what did you learn today?'

'Gosh, I don't know where to start,' she replied, taking a few moments to think.

'I learned that there are animals who breathe air, just like I do, but who live in the sea and swim under the water. But the most amazing thing I learned today was about the importance of having fun and playing.'

'Yes,' said Master Owl, 'it's all too easy to take life too seriously sometimes, so the dolphins are always there to remind us to laugh, smile and play.'

'That is so true' said Miss Bunny, nodding her head, 'it's a reminder to make the most of life and have fun.'

'Life is meant to be an enjoyable adventure,' said Master Owl smiling. 'Do you wish you had a head-nose Miss Bunny, so you could join the dolphins!?'

Miss Bunny laughed and said, 'no thanks, I am very happy being on the land and occasionally on a turtle's shell. I don't think rabbits are meant to be swimmers.'

By this time, it is late in the afternoon, and the sun is setting over the horizon. Miss Bunny had never seen the sun setting over the sea. She is totally stunned by how beautiful it looks.

The sun's rays create a golden line from the beach, all the way to the distant horizon.

Miss Bunny and Master Owl just stop and watch the sun get lower and lower in the sky, until it disappears below the horizon altogether. It starts to get dark, so they both find a comfortable spot in the sand dunes to sleep for the night.

Miss Bunny had no problem falling asleep this time. She was exhausted.

What an amazing day of new adventures, that she would never forget.

MASTER OWL'S WISE WORDS

You already know about the joy of playing. You are an expert at having fun. As you get older, there is a temptation to get all serious about life, but there is no need to take life so heavily.

Keep it light! Be more dolphin! Play for the sake of playing. Giggle and laugh. Smile and dance.

If someone doesn't have a smile, give them one of yours!

Look at all the different animals and plants on this amazing planet - some deep intelligence is playing and having fun. This deep intelligence is running through you too.

11. THE SCARED HERMIT CRAB

It is dawn on the second day of their adventures to the seaside.

Master Owl had found a large piece of driftwood to perch on for his sleep.

Miss Bunny wakes up and sees her teacher still fast asleep, so she tiptoes quietly down onto the beach and waits for the sun to rise. She loves the feel of the soft sand between her toes.

Since meeting Master Owl, she takes great

pleasure in the small things, like sitting quietly and watching the sunrise.

She loves watching the last of the stars disappear as the light starts to increase on the horizon in the east.

There was always one bright star that was the last start to disappear.

A deep crimson colour starts to rise on the horizon. The sun is painting its colours onto the clouds, just like a painter uses paint on paper.

The sea is very still.

Just a few waves gently lap up onto the shore.

Miss Bunny feels so peaceful. She cannot believe how beautiful the ocean is. She keeps thinking about the dolphins and the turtle she had met the day before.

'I wonder who I will meet today?' she thought to herself silently.

She hears a noise behind her and looks around to see who it is. Master Owl had woken up and is walking towards her.

'Good morning Miss Bunny,' he said, 'how did you sleep?'

'Morning my friend,' she replied, 'I was so tired I slept like a log!'

'That's funny,' said Master Owl, 'I slept on a log!' They both laughed.

'Did you enjoy the sunrise,' he asked.

'Yes, it was beautiful' she replied.

'What were you thinking about when you watched the sun coming up?' asked Master Owl.

Miss Bunny stays silent. She is thinking of an answer.

'That's the strange thing' she said, 'I was not thinking about anything. I was just watching the colours in the sky and enjoying the moment.'

Master Owl smiled. Miss Bunny was doing so well.

When he first met her, she had never stopped to take in the wonders all around her. She was always so busy digging and thinking. But the more Miss Bunny practiced her Magical Mindful Moments, the more she noticed how full the present moment was, especially looking at nature.

Miss Bunny notices there are shells on the beach, so she decides to go and collect some. She is enjoying the feel of the shells in her paws, when she has a big shock.

She picks up a really large shell. It is beautiful, with an amazing spiral pattern on the outside. She is just admiring it, when she hears a little voice.

'Excuse me. Can you put me down?' said the voice.

Miss Bunny looks around, to see who is speaking, but there is no-one there. Only Master Owl is around but he is some distance away on the sand dunes.

She starts walking, holding onto this shell when she hears the voice again.

'Hello, I am sorry to bother you, but can you please put me down. You are scaring me!' said the little voice.

Miss Bunny stops and looks at the shell. She

thinks the voice is coming from inside the shell, but as far as she knows, shells don't talk! But she looks closely at the bottom of the shell. To her amazement, she sees a little face looking back at her.

'Oh gosh' she said, very surprised, 'I am so sorry. I didn't know you were hiding inside the shell. What kind of animal are you?'

As she places the shell back down on the sand, the voice replies, 'thank you for putting me back on the ground. I am not hiding. This is my house. I am a hermit crab.'

By this time, Master Owl, with his very good eyesight and hearing, had walked over to Miss Bunny.

'Look Master Owl' said Miss Bunny, 'there is an animal inside this shell, called a Hermit Crab.'

'Oh yes, I have met a few crabs before, but this one is very special, because he lives inside a large shell' said the owl.

'Hello Mr Crab' he said, 'I am Master Owl and

this is Miss Bunny, my good friend.'

They listen for the voice.

'Hello' said Mr Crab. 'I am not coming out.'

Miss Bunny looked worried and said 'why not come and say hello?'

This little voice came from the shell and said 'because I am scared'.

'What are you scared of?' asks Miss Bunny.

'Pretty much everything!' replies the crab, still staying inside his shell.

They pause for a few moments. Then Master Owl said 'it's OK to be scared when we have new experiences. If you want to stay in your shell, that is absolutely fine.'

Mr Crab had never met an animal like Master Owl before. He thought for a minute about what the owl had said.

'Thank you, Master Owl,' said the crab, 'that is the first time anyone has ever said it's OK to be scared. My brothers and sisters are always telling me off for being afraid of everything.'

'Fear is a strong emotion' explained the owl, 'so we have to be gentle with it. Would you like me to help you make peace with your fears?'

The hermit crab is silent. He is thinking. Then he says, 'if that is possible, then yes please, but I have always been scared. I don't know any other way of living my life.'

'That must be very difficult for you,' said Master Owl. 'Would you like to come out of your shell, just a little bit, so I can show you something I call a Magical Mindful Moment?'

The hermit crab trusts this gentle owl and slowly pops his head out of his shell, into the sunlight. It takes a while for his eyes to adjust to the light. He hardly ever came out into the sun.

He looks up at the owl and the rabbit. 'Hello,' he says, 'thank you for helping me. What is a Magical Mindful Moment?'

'It's a chance to notice how we are feeling,' said Master Owl, 'and it can help us to understand WHY we are feeling certain emotions.'

'OK' said the Crab, 'well I am always feeling scared and I would like not to be scared anymore. I will try anything once.'

'In which case, you are already braver than you think, my friend' said Master Owl. 'Come sit with us and close your eyes. Let's all start by taking three really good deep breaths in and out.'

The three animals just slowly breathed in, held their breath for a few seconds and then slowly let it out.

The hermit crab started to feel more relaxed, with each breath in and out. He was not used to feeling relaxed. He liked it, a lot.

Master Owl continued, 'now let's just enjoy the sounds and smells all around us.'

They listened to the sound of the waves lapping onto the beach.

They listened to the sounds of seagulls squawking away in the distance.

They smelt the salty sea air, as it blew past them.

After a while, Master Owl said, 'OK, let's all slowly open our eyes and feel our bodies again. How do you feel, my friend?' he asked the hermit crab.

'So much more relaxed,' he replied, 'thank you Master Owl, I have never felt like this before.'

Master Owl and Miss Bunny smile and look at each other. Miss Bunny picks up a stick and writes 'm m m' in the sand. The letters stood for Magical Mindful Moments.

She remembered that when she first met Master Owl in the woods all that time ago, he drew the three letter m's in the earth. She had learnt a lot since then.

'So, Mr Crab' said the owl, 'can you tell me what you are most afraid of?'

The hermit crab lifts up his arm and points his claw in the direction of the sea and says, 'THEM!'

All three animals look towards the sea. At first Miss Bunny cannot see what the crab is pointing at. Then she squints her eyes as she sees something very strange on the horizon. It's a shape, with smoke coming out of it.'

'What on earth is that?' she asks her friends, 'what kind of animal has smoke coming out of it?'

'My dear Miss Bunny, that is not an animal. That is a boat. A fishing boat.'

Miss Bunny looks at Master Owl. She is very confused.

For a short while no sounds come out of her mouth at all. Her brain is not working either.

Then she asks, 'what is a fishing boat?'

The crab answers her question, 'it's a big machine that floats on the sea and is driven by humans. That is who I am most afraid of - Humans.'

Bear in mind that Miss Bunny had never left the forest before. Up until this point, she had lived in a little community of animals, in her house at the bottom of Master Owl's tree.

'What is a human?' she asks, 'are they some kind of animal?'

Master Owl smiles and says, 'yes, that's exactly what they are. But I am not sure they see themselves as animals anymore. To them, we are animals, but they think of themselves as different to animals.'

Miss Bunny was too shocked to say anything. She had never even heard of these humans before, let alone seen them. Then the questions started to arrive in her head.

'Do humans have legs and arms and breathe air like we do?' she asks, with a puzzled look on her face.

'Yes, they have two legs, just like we do' said Master Owl.

'Speak for yourself' said the Crab, smiling, 'I have 10 legs!' He moved them all around, just to make his point.

'And I have four legs' said Miss Bunny.

'Good point, both of you,' said Master Owl, 'humans have two legs, two arms and they are mammals, so they breathe air just like you and I do.'

'So, are those humans on that boat like the dolphins? Do they breathe air and live in the water?!'

Both the owl and crab smiled at each other. Poor Miss Bunny was very confused.

'No, they are not like dolphins at all' said Master Owl, 'although they can swim in the sea, but not as quickly as dolphins. This is why they are on a boat. They are catching fish for other humans to eat.'

'Dolphins also catch fish to eat,' said Miss Bunny, 'so humans are like dolphins, are they not?'

The hermit crab decides to join the conversation. 'Humans are not like the dolphins, because they do everything on such a big scale, without thinking about the consequences of what they are doing. This is why I am so scared of them Miss Bunny.'

'What do mean when you say humans do things on a big scale? I don't understand' she asks.

The crab continues, 'when the dolphins catch fish to eat, they only take a few fish at a time, so there are always enough fish to eat. They never take more than they need to live on.'

'So how do humans catch fish, out there on that boat? Do they use their hands?' she asks.

Mr Crab burst out laughing. Miss Bunny noticed Master Owl did not.

'If humans caught fish in their hands, I would not be so afraid of them, but they use things called fishing nets. They drag these huge nets through the water, in order to catch the fish.'

'Well, that doesn't sound too bad' said Miss Bunny, 'when I go collecting apples in the forest, I have a little net bag to keep them in. It's a good idea to use a net, is it not?'

'When you collect apples, you ONLY have apples in your bag' said the crab, 'but when the humans drag the nets through the water, they don't only catch the fish they want to eat, they catch so many other animals that they don't even want to eat.'

'What kind of animals?' asks Miss Bunny.

'Dolphins, whales, sharks and even crabs, like

me' said the hermit crab.

Miss Bunny had not heard of animals called whales and sharks, but assumed they all swam in the sea like fish.

'And what happens to the animals the humans don't want to catch, when they are in their nets?' she asks.

The hermit crab looked at Master Owl, who was very quiet, then he slowly looked at Miss Bunny and said, 'most of them die and are thrown back into the sea.'

Miss Bunny was so shocked, she could not move. She just stares at the crab and then looks at Master Owl.

'Can you see why I am so scared of humans?' said the crab.

'Yes, I can' said Miss Bunny, 'but I just don't understand how they can do something like that. Do they not care about all the other animals that die in the fishing nets?'

It was time for the wise Master Owl to speak. 'I

have a special name for humans. I call them The Sleepers.'

Both the hermit crab and Miss Bunny looked at him, slightly confused.

'Why do you call humans that?' asks Miss Bunny.

'Because it's like they are asleep. They do not realise what they are doing and how it affects the other animals on the planet.

Miss Bunny, do you remember when we met Mr Elephant in the forest some time ago?'

'Yes' she replied, 'he cut down all those trees and then got washed away in a mud slide when the rains came. He didn't realise that when you take away all the trees, the soil has nothing to hold it together, so it just washes away.'

'That is correct' said Master Owl, 'and once Mr Elephant realised this and made the connection between his actions and the environment, he woke up.

'So, it was like he was asleep before and then he

woke up' said Miss Bunny, starting to understand what her teacher was saying.

Miss Bunny stared out at the boat, moving slowly along the horizon, smoke coming out of its chimney and asks 'is this why you call humans 'The Sleepers' because they are asleep to what they are doing?'

'Exactly right' said Master Owl, 'but I am happy to tell you that some of The Sleepers are waking up, just like Mr Elephant did.'

He looked at Mr Crab and said, 'my dear friend, please keep yourself safe and stay well away from the humans. Miss Bunny and I have a long journey ahead of us and we must leave you now.'

'I will stay safe' said the crab, 'this is why I stay in my shell most of the time.'

'Is that so you can't be seen by the humans?' asks Miss Bunny.

'Yes, thankfully humans don't eat shells, so I am safe in here' he said.

The Hermit crab went back into his shell, with

just his legs poking out. He walked sideways away from his new friends, across the beach and down into the water. He disappeared out of view.

Miss Bunny hoped he would be safe, hiding in his beautiful shell. She turned to Master Owl and asks, 'you said we were going on a journey. What adventures are we going to have next?'

Master Owl smiled and said 'We are going on a long journey to learn about The Sleepers. It's time you learned all about the humans.'

'That sounds amazing and a little scary' she said. 'Can we help them at all?'

Master Owl loved how kind Miss Bunny was. She had such a big heart. She always wanted to help others.

'Yes, Miss Bunny' he replied, 'we are going to help them wake up.'

They stopped and took a last look at the beach. They would miss the sounds and smells of the ocean.

They both took three slow breaths in and out, to

help prepare them for the long journey ahead.

Miss Bunny jumps onto her teachers back and feels the warm feathers under her feet. She holds on tight, as Master Owl takes a few steps along the sand, opens his enormous wings and gracefully lifts up into the sky.

He climbs higher and higher, flying into the sunset.

New adventures await them both . . .

MASTER OWL'S GUiDE TO MiNDFULNESS

'Hello, thank you for reading about how I met the wonderful Miss Bunny, my new apprentice and how we helped other animals to be happier and more peaceful. Miss Bunny and I would also like to help you and your family to be happier and more peaceful as well.

Our minds are so busy thinking all the time. From the moment we wake up in the morning to when we fall asleep. Always thinking. It can be exhausting.

So taking a moment to stop and notice our in and out breaths, to notice the sounds around us, to notice our bodies and to notice how we are feeling gives us a much welcomed 'thinking holiday'. Thankfully, we don't have to travel anywhere for this little holiday!

Mindfulness helps us to notice and connect with the present moment. With the here and the now.

As you know, I call these 'Magical Mindful Moments' or 'mmm' for short, because these moments of calm are full of wonder and joy. Even after just 5 minutes of mindful breathing, you will feel calmer and more peaceful. When we come back to the present moment and notice the natural rhythm of our breathing, we come Home.

So here are my five simple steps to have a Magical Mindful Moment.

(over the page!)

1. Find a quiet space and get comfy. It can be inside your home or outside in nature. I live in a tree, so I am very lucky to be outside most the time! Close your eyes and take in three deep breaths in and out of your nose.

2. Notice your body touching whatever you are sitting or lying on. Feel your body in contact with the chair or the ground. Feel how heavy your body feels. Feel how well supported you are. Move your attention slowly from your head, down to your toes and think about how your body is feeling.

3. Notice your tummy rising and falling with every breath in and out. Notice the air moving in and out of your nose with every breath in and out. We all have this beautiful rhythm of our breathing going on inside us all the time, we are mostly too busy to notice it. It's very relaxing to notice our breathing

4. With your eyes still closed, just listen to all the sounds around you. What can you hear? When our eyes are closed, we can hear much better, because our brains don't have to process all the information our eyes provide. I love to listen to the sounds of nature. I love the sounds of birds singing.

5. When you are ready, just wiggle your toes and slowly open your eyes. Smile. Welcome home. You will feel a lot calmer.

A Magical Mindful Moment can also help us to focus more on jobs we need to do.

 Remember, whenever you are feeling stressed or worried, just close your eyes and take three deep breaths in and out. If you need to, also go and speak with an adult and share how you are feeling. As another wise person once said, anything that is mentionable, is manageable.

May you be happy. May you be well. I look forward to sharing more adventures with you...

Much love from me and Miss Bunny.'

Master Owl

ALSO BY ROB HOLMES

Master Owl meets Miss Bunny

(Picture book)

The Little Drop of Water

(Picture book)

ABOUT THE AUTHOR

Hello. I hope you enjoyed this book. I am Rob Holmes and I write children's books that combine wisdom stories and mindfulness.

Master Owl is the wise guru who helps other animals to overcome issues they are suffering with. With his apprentice Miss Bunny, they transform lives.

Before writing books, I co-founded the Gro Company, which made the Grobag baby sleeping bag and other baby sleep products. I am proud to have invented the Gro-Clock, which has been a best seller on Amazon for over a decade and sold millions of units.

I live in South Devon in the UK and spend as much time as I can on the ocean or walking the coastal path.

For more information about my books, see:

www.robholmes.org